"We can't m[ ] strangers [ ]"

There was a desperate quality to her voice, but Vasco's response was gentle. "Yes, Abby, but intimate strangers. You cannot deny that in one area at least we are compatible. And I promise next time will be even better, *cariña.*"

"You don't have to promise me anything." The color flared in Abby's face. "And I—I never want you to touch me again," Abby said shakily, knowing she lied. "If there's a baby, I'll cope. People do these days."

"Wrong, *señorita.*" Vasco's hand fastened on her arm and his gentleness was gone. "If you carry my heir, then I intend him to be born with my name. And as for not wishing to be touched—" he smiled derisively "—I intend to change your mind on that score, too."

SARA CRAVEN probably had the ideal upbringing for a budding writer. She grew up by the seaside in a house crammed with books, with a box of old clothes to dress up in and a swing outside in a walled garden. She produced the opening of her first book at age five and is eternally grateful to her mother for having kept a straight face. Now she has more than twenty-five novels to her credit. The author is married and has two children.

Books by Sara Craven

Don't miss any of our special offers. Write to us at the following address for information on our newest releases.

Harlequin Reader Service
901 Fuhrmann Blvd., P.O. Box 1397, Buffalo, NY 14240
Canadian address: P.O. Box 603,
Fort Erie, Ont. L2A 5X3

SARA CRAVEN

witch's harvest

Harlequin Books

TORONTO • NEW YORK • LONDON
AMSTERDAM • PARIS • SYDNEY • HAMBURG
STOCKHOLM • ATHENS • TOKYO • MILAN

Harlequin Presents first edition August 1988
ISBN 0-373-11097-9

Original hardcover edition published in 1987
by Mills & Boon Limited

CHAPTER ONE

THE LIFT doors slid together, and the steel cage began its upward journey with a faint lurch, which Abigail Westmore's stomach uneasily echoed.

What the hell, she thought despairingly, was she doing, acting as a reluctant messenger between her cousin and her fiancé? Why hadn't she refused—stood out for once against Della and her outrageous demands? Because unless she'd totally misunderstood the situation, the letter in her bag contained some kind of ultimatum, and was the last thing she wanted to be involved with, particularly when... Her mind closed off.

For the umpteenth time she looked in her bag to check that the letter was still there, that she hadn't, by some Freudian slip, lost it on the way here. Then she glanced at her watch, making sure that her timing was exact. Della had been most insistent about that.

'You've got to deliver it just before six,' she'd said sharply. 'So don't go into one of your dreams, Abby, and forget. Everything depends on you.'

Abby had no wish for 'everything' to depend on her, particularly when it meant delivering a message to Vasco da Carvalho which he would not want to receive.

They used to execute people who brought bad news in the old days, she thought, grimacing at her reflection in the lift mirror. Not that she thought Vasco would go to those lengths, although she suspected he had a temper, but he would be less than pleased to know that Della had been discussing the rift between them with a third party.

She could always slide the envelope under the door and vanish, she thought, then sighed. No, she had to give the letter to him in person. Della had been adamant about that too.

'And if he's not there,' she added, 'you must phone me instantly—at this number.' And she had handed Abby a folded slip of paper.

Abby had been mildly surprised. After all, she'd spent the greater part of her life, since her parents' death, sharing her cousin's luxurious home in St John's Wood. She could, she thought, be expected to remember the phone number, even if she had been living in her own bed-sitter for the past six weeks. But when she glanced at the paper later, she was disturbed to see that Della had written the number of a Paris hotel.

Although she wasn't sure why she felt uneasy. Della, and her mother, often popped across to Paris on shopping expeditions for Della's trousseau. And now that Della had learned to her fury and alarm that her future married life would not be spent in the lap of luxury in Rio de Janeiro but on an obscure cocoa plantation in Amazonia, she would probably have to re-think much of her wardrobe. But it seemed odd that she was going shopping when matters between Vasco and herself were so unsettled.

The lift halted, and Abby emerged reluctantly into the corridor, her heels sinking into the deep pile of the carpet. It was the first time she had visited the apartment block where Vasco was staying, and it was all as luxurious as she'd imagined. She could see why Della had fallen into the

trap of believing this was the kind of background
Vasco belonged to, rather than some obscure corner
of the Brazilian rain forest. She could understand,
to some extent, why her cousin had been convinced
that the cocoa bean plantation was just a temporary aberration—a rich man's whim—and that
when he was married, Vasco would cheerfully take
his place in his family's wealthy export company
in Rio, with all that implied.

Abby had never been so sure. She didn't believe
Vasco's dark, elegant good looks concealed any
such weakness of purpose. The firm lines of his
mouth, the determined set of his chin belied Della's
conviction that she could wind him round her little
finger.

And Della's shock and outrage when he had made
it bluntly clear that the cocoa plantation was his
life, and that, as his wife, she would be expected
to share it with him, had been almost comical.
Except that Abby had never felt like laughing.

She reached the door of the flat and stopped,
swallowing nervously. There was a large gilt-framed
mirror on an adjoining wall, and she looked herself
over, pushing her fingers through her fine mouse-
brown hair, silently rehearsing what she was going
to say, if he answered the door. 'Oh, hi. I was just
passing, and Della asked me...'

No, that wouldn't do, she thought ferociously.
How could she go for the casual approach when
she looked as white as a ghost, her eyes twice their
normal size?

But Vasco da Carvalho had looked at her so
seldom, she thought without resentment, that he
might think her pallor was perfectly usual.

She wished with all her heart that she could have
shared his indifference. She wished that the only

emotion he had inspired in her could have been the polite interest anyone could expect to feel for her cousin's fiancé. Only it hadn't happened like that.

She was an ordinary, practical girl. She didn't believe in grand passions, or love at first sight. If anyone had told her it could happen, she would have treated it as the joke of the year.

But it isn't funny, she thought painfully. It isn't funny at all.

She had walked into her aunt's drawing-room one evening and found him standing, with Della, in front of the fireplace. And nothing had ever been the same again, nor ever would be.

It had proved the impetus she needed to get her out of her uncle's home, however. She had made one or two unsuccessful bids for freedom in the past, only to be dissuaded by her aunt's fretful accusations of ingratitude, but this time she'd stuck to her guns. There was no way she could go on living there, seeing Vasco every day, watching Della bloom as his future wife. She had thought her hidden feelings for Vasco were her own personal secret, but she had been wrong.

That was why she was here, hanging round his door, trying to pluck up courage to ring the bell.

Della's words, and the malicious smile which had accompanied them, still haunted her. 'You either do as I ask, Abigail dear, and deliver my letter in person, and on time, or I'll tell Vasco about the pathetic little crush you have on him.'

She'd said huskily, 'That's nonsense.'

Della's smile had widened. 'Oh, no, it isn't, and we both know it. You're incredibly transparent, darling, and if Vasco wasn't absolutely besotted with me he'd probably have noticed your slavish devotion for himself by now.' She held out the letter.

'Believe me, Abby, it would give me great pleasure to point out that you're dying of love for him. It would give us something to laugh about during the long winter evenings after we're married.' She studied the strained lines of Abby's face with overt satisfaction. 'And we will be married, you know. He's crazy about me, and once he realises I mean business over this Amazon jungle fiasco, he'll come to heel.' Her lovely face took on a faintly lascivious look. 'After all, he won't want to forgo getting me into bed at last. Not that waiting was my idea in the first place, but Ina, after she'd introduced us at that Embassy party, warned me if I wanted marriage, I'd have to be a good, pure girl, and string him along, and it's certainly worked!' She giggled. 'It's been almost fun, playing the sweet little virgin, and watching him sweat. I think, if it hadn't been for his damned sense of honour, I'd have let him persuade me. Because he is beautiful, as you've managed to work out for yourself, my sweet, like some gorgeous golden-skinned animal.' She sighed. 'I bet he'll be sensational in the sack!'

Abby had winced at the crudity of it. She said in a low voice, 'Dell, if you love him . . .'

'Oh, I do.' Della's eyes gleamed. 'But I don't consider the world well lost for love. If Vasco imagines I'm going to follow him to the Amazon basin like a little submissive wife, then he can think again. The choice is his: this—Riocho Negro hellhole, or me. It's quite simple.'

Abby shuddered as she remembered. She took the letter out of her bag, handling it gingerly as if it was a time-bomb, then rang the bell, praying he would be out.

But her prayers were not answered. Almost immediately the door swung open, and Vasco stood there surveying her with frank astonishment, and growing grimness.

'Abigail?' he queried. 'I was expecting...'

'Della,' Abby supplied. She sent him a small nervous smile. 'I'm sorry to disappoint you.'

'You have not,' he told her politely. 'It is naturally a pleasure to meet you again. It is some weeks, I think...' He hesitated. 'Would you like to come in?'

'There's really no need,' she said hurriedly. 'Actually, I'm here on Della's behalf.' She held out the letter. 'She asked me to give you this.'

He looked down at the letter, and the grim expression on his face deepened alarmingly. Abby had never seen him like this. On their previous encounters, he had always been at his most charming. Now, once again, it occurred to her that he was a formidable man, and Della was insane if she imagined she could force him down any path he did not choose to go.

He said curtly, 'I think you had better come in after all, Abigail.' His hand closed on her arm in a grip which brooked no denial, and he drew her forward into the flat. She found herself in a large, comfortably furnished drawing-room. 'Sit down,' Vasco directed, indicating an enormous leather sofa.

'I really can't stay,' she protested weakly. 'I only came to deliver that and...'

'Ah, yes.' His smile was wintry. 'Abigail at one time meant "handmaiden", I think. You should not allow Della to impose on you. However, even a messenger deserves some reward. May I offer you some coffee, or perhaps you would prefer a drink.'

'Neither, thanks. I do have to go...'

'You have not been instructed to wait for an answer to that?' He pointed to the letter she was still clutching.

'Good God, no!' Abby dropped the letter on to a coffee table as if it was a hot coal. 'I think you should read it, Vasco,' she said, trying to edge past him towards the door. 'Della was very anxious that I should deliver it right now, and there's probably a reason for that.'

'I don't doubt it,' he said curtly. 'Over these past weeks I have been made well aware of the way her mind works. Do you perhaps know the terms of her message?' There was a slight derisive emphasis on the last word.

'Not really,' Abby denied swiftly and unconvincingly, a faint, betraying colour rising in her face.

'I see,' he said icily.

'No, you don't.' She punched a small clenched fist into the palm of her other hand. 'Oh God, this is so embarrassing. I could kill Della! Believe me, the last thing I want is to be—involved in any way in any—problem you might be having.'

'Thank you for the assurance,' he said sarcastically. 'But any problems are of Della's own making. In my world, when a woman agrees to marry a man, she consents to share his life, no matter where or how that life is to be lived. Your cousin knew my home, my work was at Riocho Negro. I made no secret of it.'

She gave a quick meaningless smile. 'Well, it's really none of my business. Now you must excuse me. I—I have a date, and you'll want to read your letter in peace.'

'Peace is hardly the word I should have chosen,' Vasco said with sudden harshness, making her flinch. He saw this, and his face gentled. '*Tenho muita pena*, Abigail—I am sorry. You are not to blame, after all. But you should not allow Della to use you like this.'

She shrugged lightly. 'Well, it isn't for much longer. I'm sure you'll settle your differences together, Vasco. Goodnight.'

'*Boa tarde*, Abigail.'

Reaction set in almost as soon as she was safely back in the corridor, with the door closed between them. Her legs were shaking so much suddenly that she had to stop and lean against a wall until she regained her equilibrium. Another door opened and an elderly couple emerged, the woman giving Abby a surprised and frosty glance as they passed.

She probably thinks I'm drunk, Abby decided, and, God, I wish I was!

As she waited in the bus queue, she realised it was the first time she had ever been completely alone with Vasco. It had been a tense interview, and nothing like any of the childishly romantic dreams she had occasionally indulged herself with.

Despising herself for a fool, she began, almost obsessively, to recreate him in her mind, to go over every tiny detail of his appearance. Her mind's eye dwelt lingeringly on the length of the black lashes which veiled his brilliant dark eyes, the way his hair grew back from a distinct peak on his forehead, the expanse of coppery skin revealed by the open neck of his shirt, the long-fingered, well kept hands.

She gave a little shaky sigh, telling herself that she should be ashamed. It was not only wrong but futile to allow him to fill her thoughts like this. He belonged to Della. They would resolve their difficulties with some compromise, and get married, and if she was lucky she would never see them again.

Especially now that she was firmly established in his mind as an interfering busybody, she reminded herself ironically. But it was better to be regarded as a nuisance rather than a lovesick idiot. And if Della ever carried out her threat and told him her dull little cousin had fallen for him in a big way, Brazil was far enough away for her to be spared the knowledge.

And one day, she hoped, she would wake up cured.

Although not, she was forced to acknowledge, by Keith with whom she had a date that evening. He was pleasant enough, and one of the junior executives in the company she worked for, and they shared a mutual interest in the theatre, but that was as far as it went, on her side at least.

Not that Keith ever showed any sign of wishing to become wildly amorous, she thought wryly. He was far too cautious for that, far too aware of where he was going in life. Abigail often speculated that she was being put through a series of suitability tests by him, but they were leisurely enough not to cause her any anxiety. Even if she had never met Vasco, she would still have known there was no future with Keith, or anyone else she had come across, for that matter.

Perhaps she was basically cold, she thought. Maybe in her case, still waters ran shallow, and she permitted herself her fantasies about Vasco because he was forbidden territory and therefore no real threat.

In a way, she thought detachedly, as she climbed on to the bus and settled in her seat, she would rather believe that than the other nightmare which haunted her—that Vasco would marry Della and vanish from her life, taking with him, all unwittingly, all the love, warmth, and passion she would ever be capable of, leaving her to face the future bereft and emotionally destitute.

'I found the second act rather disappointing,' Keith said, frowning. 'I thought he'd failed to establish the intruder's personality strongly enough, and, of course, the whole thing hinges on that.'

'Yes,' Abby agreed, smothering a discreet yawn. She'd found the entire production rather long-winded, and less than gripping. No matter how determinedly she tried to concentrate on what was happening on stage, her mind had kept travelling inexorably back to Vasco, and the letter she had brought him, and his reactions to it. He was a man who liked to dictate terms, not agree to them, she thought uneasily.

She'd come out of the theatre with a slight headache, and had demurred when Keith suggested going for the usual drink, but he had looked so disappointed when she'd murmured something about having an early night that she had relented.

The pub was one they often used, but it seemed extra crowded that night, with no vacant tables, so that they were forced to stand near the bar. Which was all to the good, Abby thought idly, as Keith continued to hold forth on the playwright's failure to develop his characters fully. It meant they would probably not be staying long. Keith hated standing up to drink.

The crowd shifted suddenly, giving her a new perspective of the other side of the room. Suddenly Abby seemed to stop breathing, her fingers tightening convulsively round the stem of her glass as she stared at the table right in the corner.

It couldn't be! she thought feverishly. She was seeing things. She had allowed Vasco to occupy her thoughts so much that now she was hallucinating about him, imagining that he was there, in the corner, alone.

'I don't think you're listening to a word I'm saying!' Keith's faintly indignant tones broke into her trance, shattering it, and she turned to him apologetically.

'I'm sorry—I thought I saw someone I knew.'

'Oh?' Keith craned his neck. 'He doesn't look familiar to me at all.'

'He wouldn't be. His name is Vasco da Carvalho, and he's engaged to my cousin.'

'I thought he didn't look English,' Keith commented. He gave the corner a concentrated stare. 'Been drinking heavily too, by the looks of things.'

'Oh, no!' Abby was appalled. 'He hardly drinks at all. It must be that damned letter. There must be something terribly wrong.'

As she began to move through the crowd towards his table, Keith detained her. 'Well, whatever it is, Abby, it's none of our business. Leave it.'

'I can't,' she said wretchedly. 'I feel partly responsible.'

'Don't be ridiculous.' He regarded her with disfavour. 'You want to steer well clear of him, my dear girl, especially in that condition. Although I suppose you could phone his fiancée—tell her to come and collect him.'

'She's in Paris.' Abby began to move forward again. 'Please, Keith—I must help him!'

'And I see no reason why you should do any such thing.' Keith sounded really ruffled. 'Drink up, and we'll go somewhere else and leave him to his bender.

Whatever's wrong, he won't thank you for poking your nose in, believe me.'

'You don't know how right you are,' she muttered.

'Now look here, Abby.' Keith's temper seemed to be deteriorating by the second. 'Just what's your connection with this fellow? What's this letter got to do with it?'

'I wish I could explain.' She gave him an appealing glance. 'But I can't. Nor can I just—walk away and leave him in this state.'

'Well, I can,' he announced grandly. 'If you persist in interfering, Abby, then you're on your own. I'm not ruining a pleasant evening by getting into any hassle with some drunk, whoever he happens to be engaged to. You don't know what you're taking on.'

'Then I'm about to find out.' She sent him an impatient glance. 'And I'm not asking you to be involved.'

He gave her an outraged look, opened his mouth, closed it again, then turned and stalked away. She couldn't even feel sorry.

She reached the table and sank down on the bench seat next to him. 'Vasco,' she said urgently.

He gave her a long, concentrated stare as if he was having difficulty focusing, as he probably was, she realised, as she counted the empty glasses on the table. Apart from the fact that his silk tie had been loosened and the top button of his shirt undone, his appearance was as immaculate as usual. Only that unwavering gaze, and his too-relaxed posture, gave him away.

'Ah,' he said, carefully enunciating each word, 'the little handmaiden. *Que encantamento.*' He reached for his glass, but Abby forestalled him, moving it away.

'Don't you think you've had enough?' She was aware her voice was shaking a little.

'No, *senhorita*, I do not.' The smile he gave her was almost limpid, but Abby sensed it masked an abyss of darker, wilder emotions than she had ever dreamed existed. He was angry, but that was only part of it. And although she knew the anger was not directed at her, it hurt as much as if he had lifted his fist and struck her down.

'It's nearly closing time,' she tried again.

'But they have not yet called last orders,' he said. 'See how well I have learned your English customs!'

'Good for you,' Abby said grittily, reflecting that this was one custom she would have preferred him not to know. 'The thing is, I want to get home, and it's such a hassle finding a taxi after closing time.'

Vasco shrugged. 'Then go now, and find your taxi.'

'But I hoped you'd come with me.'

'Did you, *querida*?' he drawled. 'How flattering of you!'

Abby bit her lip. 'Please don't play games, Vasco. You know perfectly well I can't leave you here like this. Della would never forgive me.'

'Now there you are wrong, *senhorita*.' He removed Abby's hand from his glass with insulting ease, and drank. 'My wellbeing is no longer any concern of your cousin.'

'Oh, God!' Abby's throat tightened. 'Vasco, you mustn't take any notice of anything she said in that letter. She's used to having her own way in everything. She doesn't realise how strongly you feel about Riocho Negro.'

'Oh yes, she does,' he said softly. 'Or she would not have offered me the choice she did. At least we both now know the strength of each other's feelings on the subject.'

'Then isn't that—grounds for negotiation?' she suggested.

'Unfortunately, no.' He lifted his wrist and ostentatiously consulted the thin gold watch he wore. 'Particularly as, at this very moment, my former *namorada* is in bed with another man.'

Abby stared at him. 'That—isn't amusing!'

'On that we are in perfect agreement. But it is no joke. The letter you were so good as to bring me made that quite clear. I was informed that unless I telephoned your cousin at some Paris hotel by six-thirty to tell her I had changed my mind, and would be content to make my home with her in Rio, she intended to meet a man called Jeremy Portman and remain in Paris with him. He apparently also wishes to marry her, and give her the kind of life I so heartlessly propose to deny her.'

'She was bluffing,' Abby insisted desperately. 'She must be. I've met Jeremy Portman. She doesn't care about him...'

'It is not important.' He lifted his hand. 'Because, in any case, I would never marry any woman capable of making such a threat.'

'Oh, Vasco, no! She's confused—unhappy. She didn't realise what she was saying—how it would affect you...'

'She knew.' His voice was flat, the short syllables sounding like a knell.

Abby tried again. 'But you love her. You have to forgive her.'

'If she had loved me in the way that I believed— had been the kind of woman I wanted for my wife, then she could not have behaved in this way,' he said, the words slurring faintly. 'Anyway, it is finished. She is in Paris with her lover, and I am going to get another drink. Forgive me if I do not, this time, invite you to join me. I prefer my own company.'

She watched unhappily as he made his way to the bar. He was walking steadily, but she knew he was already near some dangerous limit, although this was probably more emotional than alcoholic.

She was shattered by what he had told her. How totally Della had misjudged him by holding Jeremy Portman, rich, blond, and not over-burdened with brains, over his head. Abby shook her head. How could Della even contemplate marrying a man like that, when she could have Vasco?

Yet it was all too probable she had no such intention. Della undoubtedly had expected Vasco to be on the phone immediately, chastened and contrite, agreeing to everything she wanted.

She could imagine Della's increasing agitation when zero hour came and went without a word from him. She groaned silently. Her cousin was probably at this minute flying back to seek him out. If so, it looked like a wasted journey, although he might feel differently in the morning, when he'd sobered a little.

She glanced up and saw him returning, drink in hand. He sat down, directing an insolently caustic glance at her.

'Still here, *senhorita*? How can I convince you I don't need a handmaiden?' The slurring was more evident now, and his tone was an insult, but Abby stayed put.

'I've told you, I don't like being out on my own at this time of night. And you're surely not too far gone to find me a cab,' she said with a matter-of-fact shrug.

The dark eyes glinted ominously at her. 'So—the quiet mouse can roar when she wishes. If I find you this taxi, will you promise then to leave me in peace?'

'Of course.' Abby shrugged again. 'There's no point in reasoning with you when you're in this condition.'

He swallowed what remained in his glass and stood up. 'Come, then.'

It was cool outside the pub, with a hint of rain in the air. A taxi cruised past as they emerged, and Abby watched anxiously as Vasco advanced to the edge of the kerb to hail it. The fresh air was clearly having an effect on him.

When she got there he was leaning against the side of the cab, eyes closed, a faint beading of sweat on his forehead.

She was about to tell the driver to drive them both to Vasco's flat, but then she thought of the lift, the long corridor to negotiate, possibly having to search his pockets for the key, and her heart quailed. Hastily she gave her own address instead.

'What's the matter with him?' the driver jerked a thumb at Vasco. 'As if I couldn't guess,' he added grimly. 'I'm not taking him in that condition.'

'Oh, please,' Abby said urgently. 'He—he'll be all right, I swear he will.' She hesitated. 'I'll pay you double fare if you'll take him.'

'Not necessary,' the driver said. 'As long as you understand, if he's ill, I'm going to dump the pair of you, no matter where we are.'

Abby nodded. 'Agreed,' she said, then hesitated. 'Could you—help me with him, please?'

'Gawd help us!' grumbled the driver, but he left his seat.

He kept a wary eye on them both in the mirror all the way back to the quiet street where she lived, but the journey was completed without mishap. Vasco lay in his corner of the seat, unspeaking, with his eyes closed. When they arrived at their destination the driver had mellowed sufficiently to offer to help her in with him.

'Glad I won't have his head in the morning,' he muttered, as he supported Vasco's tall body up the single flight of stairs. 'Right, I'll hold him, ducks, while you get the door open.' As Abby complied, 'Now where do you want him?' He looked round the room. 'On that couch?'

'I think perhaps on the bed,' Abby said hurriedly. 'It's behind that screen.'

He gave her a good-naturedly knowing look. 'Just as you like, love, but your boyfriend won't be much good to you tonight.'

Abby bit her lip. 'He's just a friend,' she said quietly. 'Thank you for your help.' She added a generous tip to the fare on the meter, and saw him off the premises.

When she returned, Vasco was lying on top of the covers where the driver had left him, breathing stertorously. She shook him slightly, but he did not stir. Moving gently, she removed his shoes, and the silk socks beneath, then unfastened his tie, and after a struggle eased him out of his jacket.

And that, she thought ruefully, is as far as I go.

She pushed and heaved him into a more comfortable position, and arranged the bedspread over him, then switched off the bedside lamp and went back into the living area. She found a couple of spare blankets and spread them on the couch, before removing her own coat, dress and shoes and wriggling into their shelter.

The couch felt hard, and she was cramped, but if she'd been occupying a feather bed, she knew she would still not have slept. She lay staring into the darkness, thinking what a mess everything was. Della in Paris with a man she didn't really love, Vasco drinking himself into a stupor, and herself involved up to her neck once again, and no happier for it.

She didn't know how Vasco would react when he woke in the morning and discovered where he was, but she could guess. She had given him more than sufficient reason already to resent her interference.

She sighed, burying her face in an unfriendly cushion. It would be hard if she were to find herself the target for his anger and bitterness at their very last encounter, but she supposed it was inevitable.

And there was a curious, bitter-sweet pleasure in knowing that he was lying only a few yards away from her, sharing a roof with her for the first and last time, even if the circumstances were in no way what she had envisaged in her dreams.

She was glad too to know that she had been of service to him, although he was unlikely to welcome the fact.

Abigail Westmore, she thought painfully. The eternal handmaiden. And on that prosaic reflection, she fell asleep.

CHAPTER TWO

THE CRASH seemed to shake the room.

Abby sat up gasping, totally disorientated for a moment. It was early, she realised, probably not long past dawn, to judge by the pale grey light stealing in between the curtains. She struggled free of the morass of blankets and ran towards the flimsy partition which separated her sleeping area from the rest of the accommodation, her hand frantically searching for the switch of the overhead light.

As the light came on, she saw Vasco sitting up in bed, raking a hand through his dishevelled hair, his eyes blank with astonishment as they met hers. Clearly, he had woken before, because the rest of his clothes were now scattered across the floor. The bedside lamp was with them, she noticed, which explained the crash.

She said, 'Are you all right? Were you having a bad dream?'

He said *'Deus!'* and touched his forehead, wincing. 'If I am, I think it is still going on.'

'You'll have a headache—shall I get you something for it? Some soluble aspirin, perhaps?' Abby was anxious to escape suddenly.

Headache or not, Vasco's eyes were travelling slowly over her, and she'd just realised the kind of spectacle she was presenting, barefoot, and clad in fragile bra and waist slip. She didn't wait for his answer, but grabbed her robe from the chair where it was lying and fled to the bathroom on the other

23

side of the landing which she shared with the two other girls on the same floor.

When she returned with the aspirin, he was very much in charge of the situation, sitting up fully now against the pillows.

He looked out of place, almost alien in the narrow bed with its charming frilled covers, like a tiger in a rose garden, and the breath caught in Abby's throat as she made her way across the littered carpet.

She said huskily, 'Here you are,' and held out the glass, which he accepted. She bent and retrieved her lamp, noting thankfully that it didn't seem to be broken after all.

He said softly, 'Now, Abigail, where am I, and what am I doing here?'

Abby began to pick up his clothes and put them on the chair.

'You'd had too much to drink,' she said in a matter-of-fact tone. 'I didn't fancy trying to get you back into your apartment in that state, so I brought you here instead. End of story,' she added with an insouciance she was far from feeling.

'And do you expect me to be grateful for your attentions?'

'No,' she admitted wearily. 'I think that would be unrealistic.'

'I think that could describe the entire situation,' drawled Vasco, looking at her through half-closed eyes. 'Was it you who put me to bed?'

She nodded. 'As best I could.'

'I am not complaining, you understand,' he said. 'It is merely a new experience for me.'

'It's not exactly run of the mill for me either,' Abby retorted tartly. 'Now perhaps we could try and get some more sleep. It's very early.'

'Presently,' he said, almost idly. 'For the moment, all desire for sleep seems to have left me.'

'But not me.' She faked a yawn. 'If you'll excuse me, I'll get back to the couch.'

Vasco leaned across and switched on the mistreated lamp. 'Perhaps you would switch off the main light as you go,' he suggested.

'Yes, of course.' Her hand flew to the switch. 'Well—goodnight.'

'Boa noite.' His voice held thinly veiled amusement, as if he recognised her unease, and the reasons for it. 'And perhaps you would also take the glass away. I find my surroundings a little cramped, and wish to avoid any more noisy accidents which might disturb you again. I seem to have caused enough inconvenience already tonight.'

Abby trailed reluctantly back to the side of the bed and reached for the glass, but as she did so his fingers fastened like iron round her slender wrist, jerking her forward so that she fell in a tangle of robe on to the bed, and across his body.

Winded and gasping, she stared up at him. 'Are you mad? Let me go at once!'

'Oh, spare me the conventional protests, little cousin,' he drawled derisively. 'Why else did you bring me here?'

'Because I wanted to help,' Abby said breathlessly. 'You—seemed in a bad way, and I didn't think you should be alone.'

'How noble of you, *querida*,' mocked Vasco. 'I have no argument with that. I am quite ready to be consoled, as you see.'

'No!' Abby wailed. 'You don't understand...'

'I understand quite well.' The long fingers slid into the neck of her robe, pushing it off her shoulders. 'Your solicitude for me is charming, especially when you are only half dressed. You have aroused my—er—curiosity, *senhorita*. I wish to see more of you.' With cool insolence, he untied her sash so that the robe fell open completely. *'Bela,'* he said in lazy approval.

She said unevenly, 'Please let me go. Whatever you may think, I didn't intend this... I only wanted to help...'

'And so you are, *carinha*, believe me.' The dark eyes glittered down at her. With his fingertips he traced the creamy swell of her breasts above the scalloped edging of her bra, making it crazily difficult for her to breathe properly.

She must be dreaming, she thought faintly.

'You may not have intended this,' Vasco continued, making no attempt to disguise the scepticism in his voice, 'but can you look me in the face and tell me you do not want it?'

It was an escape route, she realised dazedly. A way out of this emotional minefield that she desperately needed if she were to avoid making a total and abject fool of herself.

She felt his hand release the clasp of her bra, and gasped.

'Tell me quickly.' His voice deepened in challenge. 'Do you want me to stop?'

Incredibly, shamingly, she was aware of her trembling mouth shaping, 'No.'

It was madness, and she knew it. In a few hours, Vasco would be gone from her life for ever. He was taking her because she was there, and because he thought cynically that she had thrown herself at him, and neither of those were good enough reasons for what she was contemplating. Her sense of decency and self-respect alone should be making her draw back, making her reject the sensuous, lingering hands so expertly ridding her of her remaining scraps of clothing, the warm mouth hovering tantalisingly mere inches from her own.

But I love him, she thought feverishly, and at least I'll have this to remember, when I'm alone again.

'Touch me, little one.' Vasco brushed his mouth across hers. 'Show me what you want.'

Silently cursing her total inexperience, Abby lifted her hands to clasp the broad naked shoulders, pulling him down towards her. Vasco made a satisfied sound, deep in his throat, then kissed her again, stroking his tongue along the curve of her chastely closed mouth in intimate invitation. Her whole body seemed to sigh with pleasure as her lips parted for him. At the same time she was dimly aware that he was kicking aside the concealing covers to draw her closer, so that she lay against the warm, muscular length of his urgent body.

The touch of his bare skin against her own was a wild and potent magic. Of their own volition, it seemed, her shy hands began to move, to explore and caress, discovering the realities of bone, muscle and sinew. She was beyond all fantasy already. The most her wistful dreams had ever created for her was, perhaps, a brief kiss under the mistletoe at some Christmas reunion.

Then the dark head bent towards her breasts, and Abby's head fell back as a little startled cry escaped her. Vasco's mouth felt like the brush of silk against her slender, scented curves, his tongue a smoothly sensual torment as it explored the swollen heat of her nipples. For the first time in her life she felt her whole body clench in an agony of fierce and frantic excitement.

So this was desire, some part of her brain thought dazedly. It was light years away from the kind of pallid enjoyment she had experienced from Keith's kisses.

His hands were moving, gliding caressingly over each curve and hollow, down the length of her body to her hips. He paused then, tantalising her, as his fingers traced slow, erotic spirals across the flat planes of her stomach. She lay still and pliant, letting the need, the anticipation build like a quiet storm within her.

Vasco kissed her mouth again, and this time her response was immediate, her lips parting hungrily in sensuous ardour, her own tongue moving in restless delight against his.

Her body was melting in abandonment, her slender thighs slackening involuntarily, as his hand moved again, sensually insistent, explicitly demanding. Shock jarred through her being, commingled with piercing, blinding desire.

'Touch me,' he commanded again, his voice husky.

She knew the kind of intimacy he was demanding from her, and for a moment her inhibitions rushed back to engulf her. It suddenly occurred to her that everything was moving too far too fast. She wasn't ready for this, any of it. Because no matter how wantonly her body might be reacting to the almost calculated expertise of his lovemaking, in her mind she was still Abigail Westmore, spinster.

Impatient at her hesitation, Vasco captured her hand and carried it to his body in silent exhortation. Momentarily she was stunned, shattered by her own ignorance and inexperience. Then, shyly at first, then with increasing confidence, her caresses paid homage to the strength and power of his maleness, while he murmured his enjoyment against her body.

She had at some point stopped thinking, it seemed. In place of the composed, rational being she'd taken for granted was some wild, mindless creature, wholly at the mercy of her sensations and instincts. Touching, she knew dimly, was not enough. Her body burned and ached for more, and as if he sensed her passionate desperation Vasco moved, poising himself to claim her.

His mouth took hers hungrily, almost violently, and at the same moment his body pushed into hers in stark, compelling demand.

Suddenly, horrifyingly, Abby was in pain. She cried out against his lips, her eyes dilating in panic and confusion, trying to wrench her wincing body away from him.

She thought he would stop. But he did not. Instead, his hands slid under her hips, lifting her slightly towards him as he thrust forward, subjugating her completely. She tore her mouth from his, moaning, biting at her lip.

'*Idiota!* Why didn't you tell me?' His voice was husky. 'Be still, or there will be more hurting.'

He made no attempt to move, either to withdraw, or further his possession of her. Instead he held her in his arms until the hurt-frightened trembling subsided, and she was quiescent under the imprisonment of his body.

Then, without giving her time to protest, he began to kiss her again, tiny, fleeting caresses on her face, throat and breasts. The motion of his body inside her was gentle too, coaxing her to join him in some universal rhythm.

She could feel this strange beguilement reaching for her, enfolding her, seducing her against her will, and beyond all control. But she had to fight it. Had to, or she would be lost for ever. Her mind saw this with a cold clarity. This new subtlety, this appearance of tenderness meant nothing at all. He was using her, that was all, manipulating a situation her own naïveté had created.

He didn't care about her, and why should he? She was merely a convenient body to be enjoyed, and that wasn't enough. It could never be enough.

A voice she hardly recognised as her own said, 'Stop—please!'

'Deus, querida!' It emerged as a groan of disbelief. 'You cannot mean it?' His eyes met hers in a kind of anguish. 'Are you in pain still?'

'Yes.' Her face was set and stony as she looked back at him.

He said something softly in his own language, and for a moment his hand stroked her hair back from her damp forehead. The unexpected caress almost unnerved her. It made her want to cling to him, to tell him everything she felt for him in her heart, and that was impossible.

She saw his dark face tauten, felt his possession of her quicken, deepen almost to savagery, heard a hoarse cry of satisfaction torn from his throat, and then it was over. Vasco collapsed beside her and lay breathing raggedly, his face buried in his folded arms.

Abby lay still, staring up at the ceiling. She felt bemused, cheated, every inch of her body crying out for the fulfilment she had denied it. The risk of self-betrayal now seemed small, compared with the agony she was currently experiencing, but it was still real, and his continuing presence beside her was a threat to her self-command.

Swallowing past the knot in her throat, she put out a tentative hand and touched his sweat-dampened shoulder.

'Will you go now, please?'

There was a silence, then Vasco lifted himself up on to an elbow and stared at her, the dark brows twisted in a frown.

'We need to talk,' he said brusquely.

'No!' The sound was almost violent, and Abby made a grab for an appearance of composure at least, when she saw the astonishment in his eyes. 'There's—really—nothing to talk about, and I want you to leave. Now.'

For a long moment he watched her broodingly, then the bronze shoulders lifted almost negligently in a brief shrug. 'As you wish.'

He threw back the covers and got out of bed.

For a few heart-stopping seconds Abby's eyes drank in every strong, supple line of his magnificent body, then she turned resolutely on to her side and lay, eyes closed, listening to the small sounds of him dressing.

Then there was silence, with Abby desperately conscious that he was standing beside the bed, looking down at her. She lay rigidly, eyes clamped shut, nails curling into the palms of her hands.

Let him think she was asleep, she prayed soundlessly and absurdly. Let him—just go.

At last she heard him sigh, and move away towards the door. Then his voice, quiet and almost mocking. '*Adeus*—handmaiden.'

She didn't reply, or give the smallest sign that she was aware of his departure. Only when she heard the flat door open and close behind him did she dare relax, and allow herself the luxury of her first slow, bitter tears.

She awoke late the next morning, and lay for a long time, trying to summon the energy to get up and tackle the usual weekend chores.

The other tenants were away, spending the weekend with their parents as usual, so Abby was able to spend a long time in the bath, washing her skin and her hair as if she was taking part in some ritual cleansing ceremony. As she dried herself, she inspected herself almost clinically in the mirror. It seemed impossible she should look the same after what had happened, yet she did, apart from the shadows under her eyes, and a few reddened patches on her body where Vasco's rougher skin had grazed her.

They would fade soon, she told herself vehemently. Then there would be nothing to remind her what an abject, appalling fool she'd made of herself.

For once she didn't bother to get dressed. She just put on her robe, while she started straightening her small domain, starting with her sleeping quarters. She dragged the sheets and covers from the bed, turned the mattress, and re-made the bed completely and immaculately, before embarking on a thorough dusting, polishing and vacuuming. She had to push herself to do it, but it seemed the only way in which she could exorcise Vasco's presence from the room. And she needed to do that if she was to preserve some kind of sanity.

Last night had been madness, from that first moment when she had walked towards him across the crowded bar. In some secret compartment of her mind, she'd known what would happen. She'd wanted it to happen—had created it perhaps from her own need. And now she had to block it out. Forget it.

She knew she ought to go out and buy food, but she couldn't face the thought of the bustling shopping centre, and the cheerful repartee of the shopkeepers who had become used to her regular custom. She would manage on whatever there was in the tiny fridge.

By evening the flat shone, but it had been the longest day she had ever spent, and the walls were beginning to close in on her claustrophobically.

She heated herself a tin of soup in the communal kitchen, and toasted a bread roll to go with it. She was tempted to eat there too, but the silence seemed oppressive, and eventually she carried the tray back to her flat, and had her meal by the fire. She turned on the television and sat through a raucously cheerful quiz show, before turning to a disaster movie on another channel. But the trials and tribulations of the assorted misfits threatened with total annihilation by an impending tidal wave seemed minor, compared with her own problems.

'Serves them right,' she muttered.

She was going to turn the set off, when the doorbell rang, and she stiffened. It was probably Keith, calling to apologise for his bad-tempered departure the previous night. She hadn't the slightest wish to see him, or hear any apology he might wish to make. And if she kept quiet, he might go away.

The doorbell sounded again imperiously, and she sighed. Of course. The passage was in darkness, and he would see her light shining under the door.

She took a reluctant step towards the door, then halted, as another realisation burst on her. It might not be Keith at all. It could well be Della, hotfoot from Paris, and demanding to know what had happened to her letter.

Abby's mouth felt dry suddenly, and she passed her tongue rapidly over her lips. Oh God, she couldn't face Della, or the inevitable scene that would ensue.

Now that her cousin's scheme for bringing Vasco to heel had gone disastrously wrong, she would be looking round for a scapegoat, and Abby was already too consumed with unhappy guilt to be able to cope.

The bell stopped ringing, and she drew a sigh of relief. But any hope that she was to be left in peace proved shortlived. Her visitor was now knocking on the door in a crescendo of sound which would disturb every other tenant in the building.

'All right,' she called wearily. 'Just a minute!'

As she unfastened the latch, the door was pushed determinedly from the outside, and Vasco da Carvalho walked in. He slammed the door behind him and stood regarding her grimly.

Abby's hand stole to her throat. 'What do you want?' she demanded croakily.

'To talk to you.' His tone was silken but implacable. 'Or did you really think I could be banished so easily?'

'I told you—there's nothing to discuss,' she began, but with a snort of impatience he took her arm and propelled her to the sofa.

'Sit down,' he directed curtly, walking to the television set and pressing the off-switch.

Abby's brows lifted haughtily. 'Please make yourself at home.'

He sent her a sardonic look. 'I think I already did so—don't you?' Two swift strides brought him back to her side. He seemed to dwarf the room,

she thought helplessly, and not merely because of
his height either.

He took her small, cold hands in his and drew
her down on the sofa beside him.

There was a silence, then, 'Look at me,' he ordered softly.

She obeyed reluctantly, looking up into his set,
unsmiling face, and wondering whether she felt
more wretched than foolish, and if it really mat-
tered anyway.

He said, 'Why did you not tell me you were a
virgin?'

She shook her head, allowing a defensive curtain
of hair to fall across her face. 'I—I didn't think it
made any difference.'

He sighed. 'You cannot be that naïve. Did you
imagine I would be flattered by such a sacrifice from
you?'

'I—I wasn't thinking very clearly at all.' To her
horror, a tear squeezed under her lashes and ran
down her cheek. Vasco said something soft and
pungent in his own tongue, then brushed the drop
of moisture from her face with his forefinger.

'It is too late for tears,' he told her brusquely.
'Now, we must consider what is to be done.'

'There's nothing,' she said flatly. 'I'm just being
stupid and—and female. It happened, and now it's
over, and that's all there is to it.'

'There could be a great deal more.' His voice was
quiet. 'Has it not occurred to you, little fool, that
there could be a child?'

Her breath caught. 'No—it's not possible...' Her
voice broke off in a little distressed wail.

'It is entirely so,' Vasco assured her grimly. He
paused, watching the play of colour under her deli-
cate skin, and the way her hands twisted together

in her lap. 'I blame myself bitterly, if that is any consolation,' he went on tonelessly. 'You—learn quickly for a novice, otherwise I might have suspected the truth and brought the situation to a halt before any real harm was done. But I wasn't thinking clearly either. Having discovered that your cousin was a whore, it suited my purpose to believe that you were one also.'

'That's not fair!' Abby protested.

'To you—undoubtedly not.' The dark face hardened into bitter implacability. 'To her—entirely. When I would not pay her price, she sold herself to another fool.' He shook his head. 'But that does not excuse my conduct towards you.' He gave her a measuring look. 'Although, as I have said, much of that could have been avoided if you had told me how innocent you were.'

'It never occurred to me that you'd—know.' Her gaze fell away. 'I didn't realise either what—it would be like . . .'

Vasco's mouth twisted wryly. 'As to that, I think you were a little unlucky, *querida*. And I could have made it—easier for you, had I known . . .' He paused again. '*Com a breca*, what am I saying? Had I been—warned, I would never have taken you at all.'

She still didn't look at him. 'Vasco—if you're thinking that I'll tell Della, I won't, I promise. You were angry last night, and you had too much to drink, and you said a lot of things you didn't mean. You can't just—stop loving someone, no matter what they do.'

'Whether or not I still love your cousin is immaterial,' he said harshly. 'She has made it impossible for our marriage to take place. I do not take as my wife another man's leavings.'

'You won't give her a chance to explain?'

Vasco shrugged. 'No explanations are possible. I have spent today telephoning my family and friends and telling them the wedding will not take place. I have also spoken to your aunt and uncle, who will make the necessary announcement in the papers.'

'It all sounds—very final.' Abby bit her lip. 'I'm sorry.'

He shook his head. 'You have nothing to regret. Both Della and I seem to have—used you as a pawn in our selfish games. I can only ask you to forgive me, Abigail, and allow me to make amends to you.'

'There's no need.' Her face burned. 'You see, you were right about one thing. I—I wanted it to happen...'

'Yes, I think that is true,' he said unexpectedly. 'Which encourages me to say what I must.' He took one of her nerveless hands and lifted it swiftly to his lips. He said softly, 'Marry me, *querida*. Be my wife.'

CHAPTER THREE

ABBY said faintly, 'Have you gone quite mad?'

The dark brows rose. 'I don't think so. It seems to me that my—proposition is the only sensible solution to a number of problems.'

He'd said 'proposition,' she thought, not 'proposal'.

She said, 'I suppose you're thinking about my being pregnant again.' Her chin lifted. 'Well, you have no need to worry. I—I'm on the Pill.'

Vasco's eyes narrowed. 'I do not believe you,' he said flatly. 'Now think again.'

A mutinous flush rose in her face. She stared down at the carpet. 'It's hardly likely, after all. Not after...'

'You are not merely innocent but ignorant,' Vasco said acidly. 'But as proof is beyond both of us at this time, it might be wiser to presume that it has happened. And I cannot return to Brazil, Abigail, and leave you in this uncertainty.'

She bit her lip. 'I could write to you—if the worst came to the worst.'

'Thank you,' he said coldly. 'You presume that I will then be able to drop my responsibilities to the plantation and rush back to Britain.' He shook his head slowly. 'No—when I leave, I shall not return.' The long fingers cupped her face, making her face him. 'And when I go, I intend to take my wife with me. You, *senhorita*.'

Her throat felt constricted. 'Vasco, you still love Della. It isn't too late. She doesn't want to marry Jeremy Portman, I swear it. It was just the thought of Riocho Negro that frightened her. It's so different from anything she's ever experienced. She's used to shops—theatres, restaurants. They're part of her world.'

'I know that.' His face was brooding. 'I was prepared to make allowances. But not to submit to emotional blackmail.'

'But you could meet her half-way,' Abby insisted almost feverishly. 'Couldn't you set some time limit—assure her that eventually you'll take her to live in Rio?'

'You seem to be suffering from the same misapprehension as your cousin. Understand this, Abigail. Riocho Negro is mine. It belongs to me, and it owns me too, as I tried to explain to Della. There was never the remotest possibility of my returning to live in Rio.'

'Perhaps she didn't realise,' she persisted.

'Let us be honest. Della did not wish to realise, although I explained the position over and over again.' His mouth twisted wryly. 'Now I must tell you. I inherited the plantation at Riocho Negro from a distant cousin, Afonso da Carvalho. His family had occupied the land there for several generations, growing cacao, and he wrote during one of my vacations from the university inviting me to visit him. As we had almost lost touch with that side of our family, I agreed. I was young enough to consider it an adventure.'

'And wasn't it?'

'At first, yes. Afonso was much older than myself, and had married late. His wife was very young, and an angel, expecting their first child. He had made elaborate arrangements for this important birth. Beatriz was to be taken in good time to a clinic in Manaus. Everything seemed fine.'

His face grew bleak. 'Then one morning, he was called out to look at some of his young trees. They were showing signs of disease—a fungus called witch's broom, which can only be cured by destroying and burning the damaged trees. It was a setback he did not need, although God knows he should have been used to it by that time. Ants, pests, a variety of diseases attack the trees constantly. Vigilance is always needed to protect the crop.' He sighed. 'We had just begun clearing the diseased trees when a message came from the house. Beatriz was in labour, six weeks before her time. A doctor was sent for from the settlement, but it was too late. There were complications, and within hours both his wife and son were dead.'

He shook his head. 'Afterwards, he was a different man. He seemed to lose all will to live—to fight, and I worried about him, about what he might do. I should have returned to university to take up my studies, but I knew it was impossible. Afonso needed me, so I stayed.'

'Wasn't that rather hard on you?' asked Abby. 'You were very young to be faced with such a decision.'

Vasco shrugged. 'Perhaps, but I had grown fond of Afonso, and his Beatriz. I understood his grief, and shared it. As time went by he came to rely on me more and more. He began to drink, and I found I was running the plantation with the help of his overseer. At first, I was interested in the cacao crop because I had to be, but eventually I found my interest was genuine. It presented the kind of challenge I would never have met in the comfortable, cushioned existence planned for me in Rio. When Afonso died, leaving me the plantation, I was elated. It never crossed my mind that I was free to return to Rio and take up my life there again. In my heart I had already become part of Riocho Negro. As,' he added drily, 'I tried to tell your cousin.'

'She couldn't have understood,' Abby began, but he interrupted, his dark brows snapping together.

'No, Abigail. It is you who does not understand. My engagement to your cousin is over, and I have asked you to be my wife. I am still waiting for an answer.'

There was a long silence. Abby's heart was bumping against her ribs. She said, 'It's impossible.'

'Why is that?' His eyes were fixed unnervingly on her face. She shrugged. 'Because—well, we're strangers to each other.'

'But intimate strangers, you must agree.' His grin was slow and amused, and she found her own lips reluctantly curving in acknowledgement. 'Besides, *querida*, if I'm honest, the possibility of a child is not the only consideration. My neighbours, the workers on the plantation, are expecting me to return married. To go back to Riocho Negro alone would not be a pleasant experience. In such a small community, there would be gossip—speculation.'

'And you think they'll say nothing if you turn up with the wrong woman?' Abby asked. 'Or do you expect me to masquerade as Della?'

'Of course not,' he said impatiently. 'Why do you insist on mentioning her at every opportunity?'

'Because she exists.' Abby waved a hand, rather wildly. 'You can't just—dismiss people from your life like that!'

'The decision was hers alone.' His face and voice were implacable. 'The only decision that now concerns me is your own.'

'But it seems so cold-blooded,' she protested.

'Is that what you think?' he asked cynically. 'I thought last night would have taught you differently. I am now trying to be practical, yielding to the pressure of our circumstances.' He was silent for a moment. 'Yes, we are little more than strangers,' he went on, more gently. 'But in my world, still, that is not so unusual. Besides,' he paused again, 'you cannot deny that in one area at least, we would be—compatible.'

The note in his voice, the overtly sensual reminiscence in his glance, brought the colour flaring in Abby's face. She said, stammering a little, 'I don't know how you can say that, after—after...'

'After you allowed your sense of grievance at my brutality to supersede everything else,' he said sardonically. 'But you must admit that until the moment of truth you had enjoyed being in my arms. You have admitted you wanted it to happen, and I regret that you found the experience a disappointment. Next time will be very different, I promise, *carinha*.'

'You don't have to promise anything,' Abby said shakily. 'I—I never want you to touch me again. I couldn't bear that. That's why I can't marry you, Vasco. If there's a baby, I'll cope somehow. People do these days. It isn't the stigma it once was, really...'

His hand fastened on her arm, the fingers biting into her flesh. 'And you think I can be content with that?' he demanded harshly. 'Going back to Riocho Negro in ignorance, never to know, or set eyes on my firstborn? You imagine, do you, that I have no rights in such a matter?' He shook his head. 'You are wrong, *senhorita*. If you carry the heir to Riocho Negro in your body, then I intend him to be born with my name.' He paused. 'As for your not wishing to be touched,' he smiled derisively, 'I intend to change your mind on that score.'

He pulled her to him before she could take any form of evasive action, his hand twisting in her soft hair, holding her head still, as his mouth possessed her startled lips.

She braced her hands against his chest, trying to push him away, and instead reviving the aching memory of what it was like to feel the warmth of him under her fingers without the barrier of clothing.

Almost instinctively her hands curled like a small cat's claws into his hard body, and as if he sensed her yielding, Vasco released his punishing grip to allow his own hands to slide the slender, graceful length of her spine, moulding her body against his as the kiss deepened passionately.

When he lifted his head, Abby was dazed and breathless. He had turned her in his arms so that she was lying across him, cradled on his powerful thighs. There was a faint flush along his high cheekbones, and the dark eyes glittered as they looked down at her.

'Well, *carinha*?' There was mockery in his voice, but overlaid with something rather more potent and disturbing. 'Shall I prove to you exactly how compatible we could be?'

Her eyes dilated as she looked up into his face. She was afraid suddenly of the fierce emotion his caress had engendered. And coupled with the fear was a knot of almost savage anticipation, as her passion-starved body reminded her of its frustration.

Where would be the harm? the siren's voice whispered beguilingly in her mind. Why shouldn't she give herself once more to the man she loved, let herself know fulfilment before she sent him away for ever? It might be madness, but wasn't it a greater insanity to deprive herself of the last opportunity to know the pleasure he had promised her, and which she craved?

She was at the edge of surrender, her hands lifting wordlessly to touch him, when the sound of the doorbell intruded jarringly, bringing her back to reality with a jolt.

She sat up sharply, pulling away from his gently exploring hands, dragging the loosened folds of her robe more securely round her.

'There's someone at the door!'

Vasco restrained her, his hand stroking the nape of her neck. 'They will go away,' he whispered.

'You didn't,' she said sharply, as she released herself with renewed determination.

'No, but I had reason.' He lifted one shoulder in a shrug of resignation. 'Get rid of them quickly, *querida*, and come back to me.'

That was the last thing she would do, Abby thought as she went to the door, almost tripping on her robe in her haste. The unknown caller was her salvation, a blunt reminder of the reality which lurked just outside her sensual dream world with Vasco.

Marrying him, living with him on terms of intimacy, was impossible. And letting him make love to her was equally so, if she wanted to go on keeping the secret of her love for him. When all control was gone, self-betrayal was all too probable.

If it was Keith on the doorstep, she thought as she struggled with the recalcitrant lock—or was it just that her hands were shaking?—she would have to use him somehow to get Vasco out of the flat, and out of her life.

She was rehearsing a greeting as she opened the door, but it was never to be uttered. Her jaw dropped. 'Della?'

'Yes, Della,' her cousin said impatiently. 'What the hell's the matter with you?'

Abby said numbly, 'But you're in Paris.'

'I was.' Della's lip curled. 'I've come back for an explanation. What did you do with my letter?'

'I delivered it.' Abby hung on to the door handle. 'Dell, I can't discuss it now. I'll come tomorrow and...'

'You'll talk now,' snapped Della, her lovely face mottled by an unbecoming flush. 'And you won't tell me any more lies. You never delivered that letter. I stayed by that bloody phone until midnight, waiting for him to call, so he can't have received it. So what did you do with it, you scheming little bitch?'

'Dell, go home, please!' Della was trying to push past her, but Abby blocked her way determinedly. 'Tomorrow everything will be all right again. I— I'll fix it somehow and...'

'You'll fix it?' echoed Della, rage mingling with astonishment. She took Abby by the shoulders, removing her from her path. 'What the hell makes you think...' Her voice froze into silence as she walked into the flat. When she turned back to look at her cousin, the expression of her face made Abby recoil.

'You mealy-mouthed cow,' Della said at last, her voice uneven. 'So this is what's been going on. You decided to make a grab for yourself. No wonder there was no answer when I called his apartment!'

'Della.' Abby's mouth was dry. 'This isn't as it seems...'

But Vasco's drawl cut across her stumbling. 'Why bother, *carinha*? After all, it is exactly as it seems.' He had discarded his jacket and tie, she noticed dazedly, and undone the buttons of his shirt. He was on his feet, standing hands on hips, regarding Della, his expression enigmatic.

'Vasco darling!' Della's voice throbbed dramatically. 'How could you do this to me—to us? You knew I was waiting for you in Paris...'

He shrugged. 'That is not the impression your letter gave,' he said coldly. 'In any case, I found your terms unacceptable. You wished to marry a Rio businessman, not an Amazonian cocoa planter. I wish you better fortune in your next foray into matrimony.'

A little muscle jerked in Della's face. 'But the wedding's in two weeks!'

'It was,' he corrected with a chill that seemed to penetrate Abby's bones. 'I regret the inconvenience the cancellation will cause—unless Senhor Portman can be prevailed on to take my place.'

'Darling,' pleaded Della with a sob, 'Jeremy means nothing to me. I was just saying that—to make you see how strongly I felt...'

'Then you succeeded admirably,' Vasco said tersely. His face looked as if it had been chiselled from granite. 'You have convinced me that there are differences between us which could never be reconciled in marriage.'

'But you're being unreasonable,' Della said rapidly. She was off balance now, really frightened, Abby realised with compassion. 'I want you—you

know that. Perhaps I went too far, but I'm pre-
pared to forgive your little—romp with Goody-
Two-Shoes here. Surely you can meet me half-way?'
She gave Abby a look of molten vindictiveness.

Vasco looked at her too, and his voice gentled.
'Get dressed, *querida*. I've booked a table at a restaurant for our celebration.'

'What celebration?' Della almost spat. 'What the
hell's going on here? Darling,' she swung back to
Vasco, spreading her hands appealingly, 'I've told
you—I'll overlook this. I've no doubt the little bitch
threw herself at you, and...'

'You will not speak of my future wife in those
terms.' Vasco's quiet, even words hit the room like
a thunderbolt. 'Now, it would be better if you left.'

'Wife?' Della's voice was so choked with rage,
and other emotions, it was hardly recognisable. 'My
God, you mean you're actually going to marry this
ugly, flat-chested little tart, this bloody little snake
in the grass...'

Vasco walked forward and took her by the arm.
'Allow me to escort you to the street,' he said coldly.
'Where your language belongs.' He glanced back
at Abigail. 'Get dressed,' he told her again. 'There
isn't a great deal of time.'

The door closed behind them, but she could hear
Della's voice raving on, feel the venom and rage
radiating back to her, although she could not make
out the words. She sank down on her bed, putting
her hands over her ears. This was something that
would haunt her, she thought, shivering.

It seemed a long time before he returned. She
heard the sound of the door with disbelief. Surely
he couldn't have been totally unmoved by Della's
suffering, by her open jealousy and misery?

He walked round the partition and stood looking at her, his dark face expressionless.

'Do you intend to have dinner with me in that robe?'

'You mean—the restaurant booking is genuine?' Abby scrambled hurriedly off the bed.

'Of course,' he said with faint hauteur. 'It seemed an appropriate way to mark our engagement.'

'But we're not engaged,' she protested.

'Oh, but we are,' he said softly. 'Whether you are pregnant or not, Abigail, there is no way I would leave you here at your cousin's mercy. She is ready to do you some kind of mischief.'

'I don't blame her,' Abby muttered wretchedly.

'It is not a point of view we share,' he said curtly. 'You owe her nothing.'

She swallowed. 'You don't understand. I—I grew up with her, went to school with her. Her parents have been—very kind to me...'

'Indeed?' His mouth twisted cynically. 'How odd. When I first visited their home, and met you there, I found it hard to distinguish whether you were a relative or some kind of servant.'

Abby flushed. 'Not that handmaiden business again!'

'You allowed her to use you,' Vasco said quietly. 'You will not do so again.' His hands descended on her shoulders, but she wrenched herself free.

'Why not?' she asked bitterly. 'So that you can use me instead?'

'That is not necessary,' he said. 'I have been thinking about what you said—the reservations you undoubtedly feel. So—our marriage will be on your own terms, Abigail. I have been cruel enough to you without, I think, forcing you to an intimacy you do not wish. Does that make it easier for you to agree?'

She swallowed painfully. 'On one condition,' she said at last. 'I want you to promise that if—if I'm not pregnant after all, neither of us need be held to this marriage. That we can separate, and—go on with our own lives.'

There was a tense silence. She waited, not daring to look at him.

Eventually he said tonelessly, 'Very well—if that is what you truly wish. Shall we say—six months?'

She nodded. 'That sounds—reasonable.'

'I am glad you think so,' he said courteously. 'Now, you must change, or we shall be late.'

He walked back into the living area, and after a moment she heard the muted chatter of the television.

She looked along the hanging rail which served her as a wardrobe with a sense of total unreality. She felt as if she was living through some dream, and not a pleasant one at that.

Sooner or later, she thought detachedly, she would have to come to terms with what she'd done. She had agreed to marry Vasco de Carvalho, for totally inadequate reasons, and in days rather than weeks she would be his wife, and half-way to a new life on the other side of the world.

She bit her lip. A life, she thought, for which she was no better equipped than Della. Except that in her own case she would follow Vasco over pack ice in her bare feet if he asked her.

But he would never ask, and she would never tell him. Such a confession would only be a searing embarrassment to him. He didn't care for her. He cared for the sense of honour which Della had so disastrously misjudged, and for the baby she might or might not be carrying. She looked at herself in the mirror, pressing an unbelieving hand against the flatness of her abdomen.

Could it be true? she wondered helplessly. She did some rapid calculations in her head. By the time she knew for sure, she would already be on her way to Brazil, committed to this marriage, which was no marriage at all.

She took a dress from its hanger and looked at it. It was grey in colour, silky, and subdued. Very appropriate, she thought with irony. It made her look like the shadow she was, the pale, nondescript reflection of Della's beauty and fire.

Vasco might have walked away from her, but he must feel regret for what he had lost, she thought unhappily. And if she herself had been the sophisticated, experienced creature he had imagined and wanted, he would have walked away from her too, without a backward glance, instead of being trapped by some sense of obligation.

She sighed, and began to put on her clothes, to add colour to her pale face. She had to make an effort, after all. She was going out to celebrate her engagement to the only man she had ever loved or wanted.

She was going to Brazil with him. She would live with him there, under his roof, if not in his heart. And she would have to keep her true feelings for him firmly under wraps.

But not for long, she tried to comfort herself. Six months was not a lifetime, and after that she would be free.

Once again she touched her body with tense hands, trying to divine through her fingertips whether any fundamental change had taken place.

Because if it had, she might never be free again.

CHAPTER FOUR

THE PLANE banked sharply as it turned for the approach to the airstrip, and Abby winced, closing her eyes as the treescape below seemed to tilt drunkenly.

She wasn't usually nervous about flying. She had enjoyed the luxury of the flight to Rio de Janeiro, gasping in uninhibited delight as she saw the bay, and the beaches, and the great figure of Christ brooding over the city. It was this last stage of the long journey, the air taxi which was taking them to Riocho Negro, which had aroused her apprehensions.

Not that she had any reservations about the skill of Pedro Lazaro, the cheerful young pilot. Conveying passengers and freight to out-of-the-way places, and makeshift landing grounds were clearly all in the day's work for him. But at each stage of the journey, the plane they travelled in had been smaller than the last, closing her in, reminding her, if she needed reminding, of the new and enclosed intimacy which her marriage to Vasco had imposed.

And it was the prospect of her impending isolation with him which was making her so nervous.

She'd been utterly crazy to go through with it, and she knew it. She'd known it every single day leading up to the brief ceremony which had made her his nominal wife. Her stumbling explanation to her astounded boss when she had handed in her notice had been the first humiliation. It had made her realise he had regarded her as a born and boring spinster, happy to be his secretary for the rest of his life.

And a visit from her aunt and uncle had brought a whole new set of problems. George Westmore had been uncomfortable, clearly wishing himself elsewhere, but his wife had no such reservations, and Abby had found herself bombarded with hysterical accusations and reproaches, ranging from blatant treachery to rank ingratitude. She had let it wash over her, too wretched even to offer a word in her own defence.

It had taken Vasco's unexpected arrival to put an end to the unpleasant scene. Politely but inexorably he had stopped the torrent of words, and seen the Westmores out.

When he returned, he said flatly, 'My poor Abigail. I bring you nothing but trouble, it seems.'

'But you're not happy either,' she said desperately. 'Please, Vasco—please—wouldn't it be easier to—to forget the whole thing? For you to go back to Brazil as if nothing had ever happened?'

'But it did happen.' The dark eyes hardened as they studied her pale face. 'We cannot escape that, either of us. It imposes—obligations.'

That word again, she thought painfully. Aloud she said, 'Being in love with someone else—isn't there any obligation in that?'

'I think in the circumstances, that has to be a secondary consideration,' he said icily. 'Perhaps it would be best not to refer to it again.' He took a flat packet from his coat and tossed it into her lap. 'I came to bring you these,' he said. 'Some photographs of your future home, to convince you that I am not condemning you to a hut in the jungle.'

Before she could say anything else, he had gone. Abby had looked at the pictures over and over again, until every detail of the low, rambling white building was engraved on her mind, trying to relate it to herself, and failing utterly. These pictures had been taken for Della. The house was Della's, and Abby knew that she herself would never be more than a usurper—an interloper.

She put the photographs back in their envelope and returned them to Vasco without comment, on his next visit.

He was punctilious about seeing her. He called at the flat most evenings, whisking her out to dinner, or off to the theatre, almost as if their courtship was a real one, she thought, sighing. Or perhaps he preferred to fill their time together with activity. Certainly, when they were alone together, the silences became progressively longer. She was aware of Vasco staring into space, the dark eyes hooded and brooding.

Abby obediently completed the necessary formalities for the wedding, and had the recommended inoculations. She did some necessary shopping for clothes too, choosing natural fibres in light shades and styles. But she made her choices practical and down to earth, reminding herself that she was shopping for an extended holiday rather than a trousseau . . .

Meeting Vasco's family in Rio had been an ordeal she would gladly have forgone. But it had been unavoidable, although mercifully brief. The Carvalho family had been kind and welcoming, but Abby sensed their bewilderment, their disappointment that Vasco should have chosen a wife with neither looks nor money to recommend her.

They would, she thought, have adored Della on sight. And they would have supported her whole-heartedly in her efforts to get Vasco back to Rio. It was plain that his mother in particular could not understand why he chose to exile himself at Riocho Negro. When Senhora da Carvalho had begged Abby to use her influence to make Vasco see sense at last, her smile felt as if it had been nailed on. After all, how could she tell Vasco's mother that she had no influence over him and give the poor woman something else to worry about?

'Must you go back to that place so soon?' the Senhora had mourned. 'I thought at least you would spend the night with us.'

Vasco had kissed her cheek. 'I must get back,' he said. 'I have neglected the plantation for too long already. And I wish to show Abigail her new home.'

He had almost, she thought with a pang, sounded as if he meant it.

'You can open your eyes now. We have landed.' Vasco's voice in her ear suddenly was soft, with an undernote of amusement.

'So we have,' she said weakly.

She allowed herself to be helped down from the plane, and stood watching while their luggage was unloaded. The sun was beating down, and there was a harsh, damp smell of undergrowth in her nose and mouth as she drew a breath. And from some-where near at hand came the piercing, alien cry of some unknown bird.

Abby started nervously, aware of a faint filming of perspiration on her forehead and upper lip. She reached into her shoulder bag for a tissue and dabbed at her skin, the sense of isolation already closing in. The sound of an approaching vehicle was a welcome interruption.

As she watched, a battered jeep came lurching on to the edge of the strip, and halted. The driver leapt out and came running across to them, his smile as wide as the sky, as he seized Vasco's hand and began to pump it vigorously in welcome. He was a stocky man, dressed in frayed jeans and an elderly T-shirt, and his bright eyes were alive with interest as he turned towards Abby.

Vasco brought him over to her. 'Abby, this is Agnello, my overseer on the *fazenda*. I regret that he speaks little English.'

Abby managed *'Bom dia'* as the little man shook hands ceremoniously with her, and his eyes widened in joyous surprise.

'Bom dia, senhora. Como está?'

'He is asking how you are,' Vasco translated for her. 'It's a question you will be asked many times, so I had better teach you how to reply. Say *"Muito bem, obrigada."'*

Abby complied, and had her hand shaken by a delighted Agnello all over again.

Chatting volubly in his own language, he began to heft their luggage into the jeep. Vasco listened, nodding occasionally, his brows drawn together. He lifted a hand and loosened his tie, undoing the top buttons of his shirt, as if suddenly impatient with the elegances of civilisation.

Abby thought, He's come home . . .

They were so deep in conversation that she began to think she had been forgotten. The plane started up with a subdued roar, and began to taxi to the other end of the strip preparing for take-off, Pedro Lazaro sending her a smiling salute in the process. Abby waved back, feeling forlorn as what seemed her last link with the world she knew was severed.

Vasco said with a trace of impatience, 'It is time we were going. It is some way to the *fazenda*, even now.'

It didn't matter, she thought, as she let him help her into the jeep, his hands impersonal on her slim waist. It could take months to get there, and she wouldn't care. The longer the delay, the better.

So far the whole of their brief married life had been spent in travelling, usually surrounded by other people. They had rarely been alone together. But when they reached the *casa grande*, that would change, and the knowledge was disturbing.

Until now Vasco had kept his word scrupulously about their relationship. The only physical contact between them had been the brief kisses on her hand and cheek when he took his leave of her, and he had only bothered with those when other people had been present.

Nevertheless, the fact remained that in this wild corner of the world, they would be thrown more into each other's company than hitherto.

Not that they would be completely alone. There would be the servants, of course. He had included photographs of them in the batch he'd given her, and she had tried to memorise the names written on the back, trying not to think, as she did so, that all this trouble had been taken for Della in an attempt to reconcile her to life at Riocho Negro. Her time at the *fazenda* might be limited, but while she was there, she would do her best to act as mistress of the house, she thought determinedly.

And there would be a limited social life with the neighbouring families, Vasco had told her. Her arrival would probably be used as an excuse for a party, and they would have to entertain in turn. He had glanced at her almost enquiringly as he told her, as if silently asking if she was able to cope with this kind of demand, and she had returned his gaze tranquilly enough.

She had been used to helping her aunt organise parties and dinners when she lived with the Westmores, Della having always refused point blank to exert herself. Now it seemed as if that experience, at least, would stand her in good stead.

Hard work, activity was what she needed to fill her days, she told herself robustly. She deliberately closed her mind to the problem of how she would spend her nights.

It was a hot uncomfortable journey. The road through the clustering forest was poor and full of potholes.

'It is government policy,' Vasco told her ironically, 'to improve communications in the interior. Nearly all passenger and freight traffic still goes by water.'

'I wish we could have travelled on the river,' Abby said. 'I read about it, and it sounds——' She hesitated, because she'd been going to say 'romantic' and hastily substituted 'fascinating' instead.

'Fascinating for tourists, no doubt,' Vasco said drily, reminding her with a swift glance that as the wife of a Brazilian, she could not consider herself in that category.

It silenced her. He had whisked her here, she thought wistfully, giving her little time to adjust to her new surroundings. She suppressed a little sigh. Well, when her six months was over, and she was free again, she would take the time to be a tourist, and have a long look at Brazil before she left it for ever.

The jeep rocketed along, Agnello obviously being trained not to linger over unfriendly terrain, and

Abby rocketed with it, her small weight no counterbalance for the vehicle's lively motion. She was beginning to wonder if there would be an inch of her left unbruised, when her husband's arm went round her suddenly, clamping her to his side, and robbing her of breath for more than one reason.

Agnello sent them a twinkling sideways glance, and a comment which she was glad she could not translate. She sat rigidly within Vasco's encircling arm, blindingly aware of the warmth of his body, and the strength of the long thigh touching hers.

She tried instead to concentrate on the flying scenery. If she had expected dense jungle, she was wrong. The trees were taller than she had imagined and more widely spaced than she had visualised, allowing the sun to dapple through their sheltering leaves on to the thick undergrowth.

The jeep swerved again, and the trees closed round them and over them like some high green tunnel, at the far end of which a bright blaze of sunlight waited. Vasco's arm tightened on her almost imperceptibly, and he murmured something under his breath, his tone undeniably jubilant, alerting Abby to the realisation that they were nearing journey's end at last.

Nervous as she was, battered as she felt, she was conscious of a small stir of excitement deep inside her. She might be an intruder—the wife which circumstance had forced on him—but she was *there*, beside him, about to take possession of her new domain.

As they hurtled into the sunshine, Abby caught her breath. The photographs had not done the house and its setting any kind of justice. It was set on the crown of a small rise, rearing, it seemed, out of a sea of flowers. There were other buildings at a distance, but she barely glanced at them, and even farther away she glimpsed the shimmer of dark water.

The jeep slowed, and she noticed another vehicle, a car, parked at the foot of the rise. Agnello turned to Vasco and addressed a remark to him. Vasco nodded, his face expressionless.

He looked down at Abby. 'We have our first visitor,' he told her coolly.

'Oh,' Abby said rather faintly. She had enough new and startling impressions to cope with already. Strangers, especially when she felt hot, dusty and cramped, were surplus to her requirements.

She allowed Vasco to help her down from the jeep, and stood for a moment flexing her shoulder muscles cautiously, as she surveyed the long shallow flight of steps which wound its way up to a shady veranda.

'Would you like me to carry you?' asked Vasco, and she started, swift colour burning her face.

'No, I can manage,' she stammered.

He shrugged. 'Perhaps, but isn't it traditional in your country for the bridegroom to carry his bride over the threshold of her new home?'

'Yes.' She kept her voice light with an effort. 'But this is Brazil, and I'm sure there's a different tradition here.'

'You are probably right.' The dark face was sardonic. 'But as I have not been married before, I regret I am no expert on the matter.' A note of amusement entered his voice. 'I see a reception committee is forming!'

Following his gaze towards the house, Abby saw that three women had emerged and were standing on the veranda, smiling and nodding. And men were appearing too from the buildings she had noticed, and from the encircling trees, all very casual-seeming, yet converging purposefully on the jeep and its passengers.

'They've come to look at you,' Vasco informed her quietly. 'Smile at them, *minha esposa*. Wave your hand.'

Abby obeyed, feeling absurdly shy under the scrutiny of so many interested dark eyes. Vasco spoke briefly to them, but the only words she recognised were 'Dona Abigail'. When he finished there was applause, and Abby's flush deepened, especially when Vasco's hand captured hers and he began to walk with her up the steps to the house.

'We shall have to give some kind of celebration for the workers and their families,' he said casually. 'The marriage of their *patrão* is an occasion in their lives, and as we robbed them of the actual ceremony, we shall have to make it up to them in some other way.'

'I suppose so,' she agreed in a subdued voice.

As they reached the veranda, Abby cast her mind desperately back to the photographs Vasco had shown her, trying to match names and faces. The plump older woman was Rosa, the cook, she knew, but the younger girls, their dark hair piled up into identical glossy coronets, their round faces shining with goodwill, seemed practically indistinguishable.

She decided to take the plunge, greeting the first one with a smiling, '*Bom dia*, Ana.'

Her educated guess had been spot on, she realised, and the girl giggled with surprised delight, her hands twisting in her white apron. Abby saw Vasco's brows lift, and hoped he was impressed. As she moved on to greet Maria das Gracas, she felt she had successfully negotiated an important hurdle.

As Vasco took her arm to guide her into the house, there was a raucous cry of protest, and Abby jumped, thinking guiltily that she had overlooked someone. Then she realised Vasco was laughing.

'I did not think I should be allowed to get away with it,' he said ruefully. 'Meet the real *fazendeiro* here, Abigail.'

On an elaborate perch in the corner was the biggest most brilliantly coloured parrot Abby had ever seen. As they approached it squawked rowdily again, putting its head on one side and giving them an openly malevolent look.

'This is Don Afonso.' Vasco gently scratched the great bird's head with his forefinger. 'He has lived here for a long time, and does not care to be ignored. Make his acquaintance slowly, and he will be your friend. Rush him, and you will probably be bitten.'

Abby kept her hands at her sides, and inclined her head gravely.

'*Bom dia*, Don Afonso,' she said solemnly. She made a discovery. 'He isn't tethered!'

'I told you—this is his home.' Vasco smiled faintly. 'He was caught as a chick and tamed by some Indians. Later they made a gift of him to my cousin, who discovered after a few weeks that each time someone called him by name, the macaw responded. He had no choice but to christen the bird officially as his *alter ego*.' He paused. 'Now we had better go and greet our visitor.'

Abby allowed herself to be shepherded into the house. She found herself in a broad central hall with doors opening off both sides. A large fan hummed in the ceiling, and she glanced at it in surprise.

Vasco nodded, as if she had spoken her query aloud. 'We make our own electricity.' He walked over to an imposing pair of double doors and opened them. He said in English, 'Luisa—how kind of you to welcome us like this.'

The visitor laughed musically, getting out of her chair. 'But how could it be otherwise, my dear Vasco?' she responded in the same heavily accented language. 'I could not control my impatience to meet your wife.'

If anything could have underlined for Abby that Riocho Negro was not the wilderness she had anticipated, it was the appearance of the woman confronting her. She was of medium height, her slimness accentuated by the chic black dress she wore, her glossy dark hair coiled expertly into an intricate chignon at the nape of her neck. The large shady hat discarded beside her probably accounted for the exquisite creaminess of her skin, and the shape and brilliance of her almond eyes were heavily accentuated by cosmetics. Curved scarlet lips were parted in a smile as she took Abby's hand.

'You will pardon the intrusion, Senhora da Carvalho,' she said. 'I am your nearest neighbour, Luisa Gonzaga. In a scattered community like ours, it is wonderful for me to have another woman living so close. I wanted to be the first to say *"Seja bem-vindo"*. Welcome to Brazil.'

The words, the smile, the charm were stunning, and Abby felt herself dazedly returning the pressure of Senhora Gonzaga's fingers, and murmuring something inadequate in response.

'You are a little overwhelmed, I dare say,' the Senhora went on. 'You speak our language, perhaps? No? Ah, that is a difficulty. So much to learn, when there is already a different environment—so many new faces...'

'Abigail seems to take new faces in her stride,' Vasco interposed drily. 'She has already captured the servants' hearts by knowing their names without prompting from me.'

'Ah!' The Senhora clapped her hands. 'But that is most clever!' She sounded radiant about it, and Abby had no idea what could have given her the impression that her true feelings were totally different. Jet lag, she thought, giving her hallucinations.

There was something else in the beautiful face—a sudden curiosity, a sharpening of the eyes. 'You say your wife's name is Abigail, my dear Vasco? But I thought——' She paused artistically. 'Ah, no, of course I am mistaken. It is my deplorable memory.'

Abby felt herself go hot and cold all over. It had been absurd to hope that no one would spot the discrepancy in the names, she thought, not daring to look at Vasco.

Her husband said smoothly, 'I am not surprised you are confused, Luisa. It has all happened so quickly that I can hardly believe it myself.'

'A true romance,' Senhora Gonzaga said with that relentless gaiety. 'I warn you, Dona Abigail, all the local beauties will be waiting to scratch your eyes out!' She sent an arch smile at Vasco. 'We should have kept you here, *amigo*, and not permitted you to go on leave to Europe, and lose your heart.' Her eyes swept Abby from head to foot, making her shockingly aware that there was suddenly no amusement in them at all, although her red lips still smiled. 'Such a surprise for us all!'

It was that look, and the note in her voice, which told Abby quite unequivocally that behind the smiles, Senhora Gonzaga found her neither chic, witty, or even remotely attractive. And she knew too that she was intended to know it.

'So, how do you like your new home?' the Senhora went on, all friendliness again, making Abby wonder whether she had been imagining things after all.

'I haven't seen a great deal of it yet.' Abby had been looking round the big room they were in, absorbing its atmosphere of quiet, rather shabby comfort. The furniture was clearly old, made of some rich-coloured dark wood which she did not recognise, and the chairs and sofas were covered in a subdued dusky pink fabric which showed distinct signs of wear.

'You will naturally wish to make changes,' the Senhora remarked, following her gaze. 'If I can help, you have only to ask. I would be happy to assist—advise. This could be a truly gracious home, but it has lacked a woman's touch for so long.'

Abby was tired, but she knew when she was being patronised. Perversely, she allowed her eyes to widen. 'Have the maids only just come here to work, then?'

The Senhora's radiance dimmed a little. 'I meant—the house has lacked the hand of a mistress—the eye of an artist.'

'I see,' Abby said with deceptive meekness. 'I only hope I can live up to all these expectations.'

Vasco looked at her, his eyes narrowing. 'I think the long journey has wearied you, *carinha*,' he said softly. 'If you will excuse us, Luisa, I think my wife should go to her room and rest. You will dine with us soon, I hope?'

'I should be delighted, but you must be my guests first.' The Senhora extended her hand. '*Adeus*, Dona Abigail. I am so happy to know I have another friend in this house. I have grown so much to depend on Vasco in the past sad months. It would have grieved me if his marriage had robbed me of his kindness and support.' There was another smile, wistful and appealing, a whisper of silk, and she was gone, leaving a whiff of expensive scent hanging in the air.

When husband and wife were alone, Abby looked down at the polished wood floor. 'You said something about going to my room,' she reminded him in a low voice.

'Presently,' he said grimly. 'This is a small community, Abigail, and it is not wise to antagonise one's neighbours. Dona Luisa speaks your language, and is not a great deal older than yourself. She wishes to be your friend.'

'Does she?' Abby felt weary to death suddenly. 'Well, I'll have to take your word for that, as I've only just met the lady. But I got the impression that the friendship she's so keen on is yours.'

'That is hardly surprising,' he said impatiently. 'João, her husband, died suddenly last year, just before their cacao crop was due to be harvested. Naturally, I helped with the other neighbours, but as I live nearest to her, Luisa has grown to rely on me more.'

'Oh, I'm sorry.' Abby wished she could have said that with more sincerity. 'Has she any children?'

Vasco shook his head. 'Their *fazenda* has been inherited by João's younger brother Gerulito, but he is unfortunately totally lacking in experience. Luisa has been forced to hire a manager—an

American—to run the estate while Gerulito learns his lessons.'

'That must be a difficult position for him,' Abby said slowly.

'It is. I had much the same experience myself, but at least I had the aptitude—the will to learn.' Vasco shook his head. 'I am not sure this is the right life for Gerulito. Before this happened, he was learning to be an architect in Sao Paulo.'

'Quite a contrast,' Abby agreed.

Vasco gave her a swift glance. 'But this is no problem of yours, Abigail. I'm sorry. I wished to explain a little about Luisa, that is all. Now, come and rest.'

The bedrooms were at the rear of the house, built along another full-length veranda. The room Vasco took her to was large and airy, with the inevitable fan whirring gently on the ceiling, and the windows guarded by mosquito screens. It was dominated by the big four-poster bed, a beautiful piece of furniture, made from the same dark wood she had noticed previously, ornately carved. It had other less conventional decorations too. The huge snowy pillows were surrounded by flowers, and other blooms were heaped on the coverlet.

Abby swallowed. 'Is there a shortage of vases?' she asked, with a feeble attempt at humour.

Vasco's mouth tightened. 'The flowers are a goodwill gesture from the maids,' he told her. 'I will have them cleared away.'

'Oh, no,' Abby protested. 'I wouldn't want to hurt their feelings. It all looks—very pretty.' She found she was staring as if mesmerised at the bed, taking in the significance of the pillows arranged so invitingly side by side.

'Nevertheless, you cannot be expected to sleep in a garden.' Vasco's tone was faintly crushing. 'And at the same time, I can tell Ana to make up the bed in the dressing-room.' He strode across the room and threw open another door, turning to her almost challengingly. 'You see? There is no need to look so alarmed. I am a man of my word.'

'I wasn't,' Abby said unhappily. 'I mean—I never doubted...'

'Didn't you, *minha esposa*?' he drawled. 'How very trusting of you! Now, I'll find Ana and cause a sensation in the household.' He pointed at yet another door. 'Our bathroom, *querida*, which I regret you must share with me. Make yourself at home, *faz favor*.'

Abby bit her lip, sinking down on the edge of the bed. It might look old-fashioned, but the mattress was as modern as she could have desired.

She leaned back a little, then sat up with an exclamation as her hand encountered a solid object.

'What's this?' She regarded it doubtfully. It was a wooden carving of a fist, a clenched left hand, with the thumb sticking up between the index and middle fingers.

'More goodwill,' Vasco said ironically. 'It's for you, Abigail—a *figa* to protect you against the evil eye, and bring you luck. It only works when it is given as a present, and Maria's father is a woodcarver, which explains where it came from.' He paused, then added drily, 'It has other symbolism too, which is why it was left on the bed for you to find.'

Abby said in a hollow voice, 'Oh,' as a wave of embarrassed heat swept over her.

'Oh, indeed,' he agreed mockingly, then vanished on to the veranda, calling to Ana as he did so.

Abby went on sitting on the edge of the bed, cradling the *figa* in her hands, not knowing whether to laugh or cry. Even if the present was inappropriate, she could appreciate the kindness which had prompted it. And the flowers too, she thought, reaching out a hand and picking up one of the blooms to lift to her face,

But to her disappointment, its beauty was purely visual. It was totally scentless, she realised, letting it drop back on the coverlet.

A cheat, she thought. Like me—in this house.

By contrast, the little *figa* felt warm and solid and real as it rested in her lap. She touched it tentatively, wryly. It occurred to her that she was going to need all the luck she could get if she was to survive the pitfalls of the next months.

She sighed. And sleeping night after night in a bed intended for lovers, knowing that Vasco was lying only a few yards away, was going to be the greatest pitfall of them all.

CHAPTER FIVE

ABBY woke slowly, her body uncurling into a stretch of sheer luxury as the clouds of sleep cleared from her mind. She glanced idly at her watch, then sat bolt upright in shock. It was nearly midday!

She sank back against her pillows with a stifled groan. So much for all her good intentions, she thought grimly. She'd made all kinds of plans in her head for this first day at Riocho Negro, exploring the rest of the house, and visiting the kitchens among them. And she had hoped too that Vasco would offer to take her on a guided tour of the estate so that she could find out at least the basics of the cacao industry.

The oddly subdued atmosphere which had hung over the household during the latter part of the previous day had shown her quite clearly that she had proved a disappointment in one way at least. Vasco's orders about the sleeping arrangements had been carried out to the letter, but Abby was conscious that, afterwards, the smiles from the servants were not as ready as they had been.

A newly married couple who chose to sleep apart were obviously a total bewilderment to the household. Abby had no idea if Vasco had offered his staff any kind of explanation, but she suspected glumly that they would still regard it as some deficiency on her part.

But she badly needed to make a good impression in other ways. If she could contribute to the running of the house, in spite of the language barrier, and take an intelligent interest in the work of the plantation, surely she could make up for the fact that she wasn't the girl her husband wanted in his bed, or his life.

As she pushed back the cover the door opened slightly, and Ana peeped cautiously in. Abby's pantomimed regret at having slept so long was answered with a reassuring smile, then Ana went over to the massive carved wardrobe and opened the door.

While she had rested, half-sleeping, the previous day, Abby had been vaguely aware of Ana moving about quietly, unpacking for her. Now, her attention fully alerted, she leaned forward, her jaw dropping.

The modest selection of clothes she had brought with her would only have occupied a small percentage of the space available, whereas the hanging rail was crammed with garments. Cool day dresses in cotton and lawn, she saw incredulously, as well as silk and satin and an array of cotton jeans with toning shirts and tops.

Ana was removing an ivory silk robe, which in no way resembled the simple cotton kimono Abby had packed in her case. As the girl held it out to her, Abby shook her head.

'Não,' she protested as forcefully as possible, pointing to herself. 'Not—mine,' she enunciated carefully, trying to get her meaning across.

Ana's face was blank with astonishment. She burst into a flood of excited gabble from which Abby managed with difficulty to elicit the words 'patrão' and 'Manaus'.

Della's clothes, Abby thought bleakly, as she marched to the wardrobe and found her own dressing-gown. Vasco must have organised them as a welcome present for her, and forgotten about it in the aftermath of their separation. Well, she wanted no part of them. She might have stepped into Della's shoes, but she was damned if she was going to wear dresses chosen for her too!

Deliberately she selected one of her own, a simple shirtwaister in a soft shade of green, and by no means as well made or stylish as the garments Ana was trying to persuade her into. But Abby shook her head with cool determination, indicating, as she put the dress down on the bed, that this was her choice, and no other.

By the time she had bathed in the huge old-fashioned tub in the bathroom, and put on her clothes, she felt calmer. Ana was waiting anxiously in the bedroom with offers of breakfast, but Abby refused gently, asking carefully for just coffee.

Left to herself, she made her way to the veranda at the front of the house and stood looking round her. The place seemed deserted, but her arrival yesterday had shown how deceptive that could be.

She sat down on one of the cushioned chairs, nearly jumping out of her skin as a strident squawk rent the air.

'Not deserted at all,' she said aloud, as she recovered. 'I apologise for overlooking you, Don Afonso.'

The great macaw gave her a look of undisguised hostility, then lifted one set of formidable claws and began to give them a minute examination.

Rosa came bustling out with a tray, and Abby saw with resignation that she had provided cake and some slices of papaya to accompany the coffee.

She watched maternally as Abby poured some of the dark aromatic brew into a cup, and sipped, nodding her approval before vanishing back into the house. Abby had eaten her papaya and refilled her cup, when she heard the sound of an engine.

She thought breathlessly, Vasco, and her hand went up nervously to push at her soft hair. So she wasn't going to spend the entire day alone, after all. He had come back for her, and this was a whole new beginning, she thought, her heart thumping.

But the man who jumped down from the small truck and came striding up the steps was a total stranger, tall and blond. He smiled easily at Abby, showing very white teeth.

'Hi,' he said. 'I hope I'm not pushing in any, but I'm looking for Vasco.'

Abby returned the smile rather reservedly. 'I'm Abigail da Carvalho,' she said, flushing a little as she spoke her new name aloud for the first time. 'I'm afraid I don't know where my husband is at the moment. Perhaps the servants might be able to help.'

'Maybe they could at that.' He extended a hand. 'I'm Link Dalton. I'm running the Gonzaga place on a temporary basis—until the kid finds his feet, that is.'

'Yes, Vasco mentioned something about it,' she said. 'Would you like to sit down?'

His grin widened. 'All the time, lady, all the time. This humidity gets me down. How about you?' He threw himself into the chair beside her, stretching his legs out in front of him.

Abby shrugged. 'I haven't been here long enough to judge,' she said. 'It certainly isn't as bad as I expected. I thought—oh, heavens, I don't know— that it would be much *wilder* with exotic animals, and snakes, and insects everywhere.'

'Oh, there are plenty of those,' he assured her. 'You can't judge the locality by this civilised little corner. People have been farming the area around the Little Black River for generations, and it sure makes a difference. But you only keep the forest at bay. You don't banish it completely.'

'Would you like some coffee?' Abby belatedly remembered her duties as a hostess.

'Why not? I'll shout Rosa for another cup.' He got up briskly and disappeared into the house, returning a few minutes later, cup and saucer in hand. 'The girls say Vasco will be back for lunch.' He squinted up at the sky. 'Mind if I hang round till then?'

'Of course not.' Abby paused. 'To be honest, I was beginning to feel a bit like a deaf mute,' she confessed ruefully. 'I need to learn Portuguese, and fast!'

'Get Vasco to compile a list of useful words and phrases,' her companion suggested, taking the coffee she poured for him with a brief word of thanks. 'I'm surprised he didn't think of it.'

'I think he was keen to get back to the plantation,' Abby said. 'He—he's spent a long time away from it recently, so he's bound to be busier than usual.'

'Let's face it, the guy's a workaholic.' Link flashed her an amused look. 'If I'd just got married I'd be right here, paying my bride some attention, not staring at a heap of cocoa beans!' He drank his coffee and set down the cup. 'That was some lightning romance you had there. We were all glad he decided to take a European vacation—he's been working himself into the ground here—but we didn't expect him to wind up engaged. No one had him down as the marrying kind, at least not yet.

You won't be a hit with the available chicks round here.'

'Including your employer?' The words were out before she could stop them, and Abby could have bitten her tongue in vexation.

Link appeared to give her outrageous question serious consideration. 'The Black Widow? Could be—although the lady claims her heart's in the grave. But there has to be something keeping her here.'

'I wasn't serious,' Abby said hastily. 'She—she's just so—glamorous.' She plunged for a change of subject. 'What brought you to Brazil?'

'An interest in agriculture, basically.' Link leaned back in his chair, his arms folded behind his head. 'I was doing research into the fungus diseases which attack trees, and I fetched up here eventually. It's a good enough place to be.'

'I suppose so,' Abby agreed, with a little stifled sigh.

'You sound as if you need convincing.' He gave her a lazy look. 'I'll have to see what I can do. Next time I go into town I could take you with me. Sometimes they show old movies in a tin shack. How do you go for *Some Like it Hot* dubbed into Portuguese?'

She laughed aloud. 'It sounds wonderful! Thank you very much.'

'*Não importe*. In fact, my pleasure.' He put out his hand, and this time his fingers closed warmly round hers, in contrast to the formality of his earlier greeting. 'Welcome to Riocho Negro, *senhora*.'

Abby smiled at him shyly, returning the pressure of his hand. It was oddly comforting to know that here was a potential friend—and one, moreover, who could speak her language.

Vasco's voice said coldly, *'Bom dia*, Link. Is there something I can do for you?'

Abby jumped. She had no idea where he'd come from, but here he was suddenly standing on the veranda steps, hands on hips, watching them. He was wearing close-fitting khaki cotton pants, and matching shirt open almost to the waist, and marked with patches of sweat.

Link released Abby's hand unhurriedly and stood up. 'Hi, there,' he said casually. 'I called over to replace that spray we borrowed a while back. Luisa thought you might need it.'

'That was considerate of her,' said Vasco, after a pause. His voice was level, but lacking in cordiality. 'Was that all you wanted?'

Link moved his shoulders in a negligent shrug. 'Oh, I thought I might congratulate the bridegroom on his good taste.' He smiled. 'Abigail, eh? A nice old-fashioned name, for a nice old-fashioned girl.' He frowned as if in sudden perplexity. 'Only I seem to remember another name being mentioned—now what was it? Della, or something?'

Abby felt cold. She looked woodenly at the used cups, wondering how many more of these moments she would have to endure.

Vasco said pleasantly, 'That is the name of Abigail's cousin. It is easy to see how the confusion has arisen.'

'I guess so,' Link agreed easily. 'So, how about this spray? You want that I should give it to Agnello?'

Vasco nodded. 'If you will. He is over by the drying sheds.'

'I'll drive over there, then.' Link started down the steps. He turned and sent them both a slanting smile. 'I guess you two want to be alone to enjoy lunch for two.'

'Later.' Vasco flexed his shoulders, easing the collar of his shirt away from his neck with a casual hand. 'I'm going to take a shower first.' He reached down and pulled Abby up from her chair, smiling into her startled eyes. 'Come and keep me company, *querida*.'

'Lucky bastard!' Link threw laughingly over his shoulder.

As Abby moved towards the house, compelled by Vasco's inexorable arm round her waist, she heard the truck drive off. As they reached the door she pulled herself free.

'Will you kindly tell me what's going on?' she demanded angrily.

'Not here,' Vasco said grimly. 'If you wish to quarrel with me, please wait until we are in the privacy of our room.'

Abby hung back, nervousness drying her mouth. 'I—I don't want to go to my room,' she said huskily.

'You would prefer me to carry you?' His dark eyes glinted at her. 'A romantic scene to gladden the servants' hearts, perhaps?'

'No.' She threw him a mutinous look. 'I can walk.'

'Walk, then,' he said shortly, and she went ahead of him, her chin tilted defiantly.

When they were alone, she faced him with a coolness she was far from feeling. 'Is this some kind of game?'

'How odd,' said Vasco, closing the door behind him. 'I was about to ask you the very same thing.' He was smiling slightly, but there was no amusement in his eyes. 'I did not expect, I confess, to find you on your first day here not only entertaining a stranger, but permitting him familiarities.'

'I was doing nothing of the sort!' Abby protested hotly.

'You consider allowing him to hold your hand a matter of common courtesy, perhaps?' he enquired glacially. 'I must tell you, *minha esposa*, that you are wrong. Although remembering how generously you gave me your favours, I suppose I should have expected such behaviour from you,' he added unforgivably.

Bright spots of colour blazed in Abby's pale cheeks. 'How dare you!' she said chokingly. 'Oh, God, how dare you? You know quite well...' She paused, taking a grip on herself. When she could control her voice, she said, 'Mr Dalton came here to see you. I offered him coffee because I thought it was what you'd want me to do. He was kind and friendly, and he could see I felt—strange, and I was grateful to him, that's all.'

'Then you demonstrate your gratitude rather too openly.' There was no softening in his manner. 'As my wife, you should be more discreet.' His mouth curled a little. 'For a girl who claims to be deeply in love, you seem very ready to find consolation.'

Abby felt as if all the breath had been knocked out of her body. She stared at him wordlessly, her tormented eyes questioning, wishing only that the ground would open up and swallow her.

'You thought I did not know?' he asked cynically. He shook his head. 'Alas, no, *carinha*. Your cousin was—most explicit.'

He'd taken Della down to her car, Abby remembered, hearing in her mind Della's raised, tearful voice. In spite of her distress she had taken her revenge, betrayed Abby's pitiful secret.

She found a voice somewhere. 'I'm sorry. I—I never meant you to know...'

'I realise that.' Vasco sighed irritably, raking a hand through his black hair. 'Nor did I intend to tell you, only...' He stopped abruptly. '*Deus*, what a mess!'

'Yes,' Abby said faintly. She couldn't look at him, suddenly. She should have guessed what Della would do, she thought wretchedly. It was only what her cousin had threatened, after all. She forced herself to speech again. 'Please believe me—it really needn't make any difference. We made a bargain, and I'll stand by it.' She paused, biting her lip. 'It—it doesn't have to be an embarrassment to you, I swear...'

'Embarrassment is hardly the word I would have chosen.' His voice bit, making her flinch. He must have seen this, because his tone gentled. 'And you are naïve, Abigail, if you think it makes no difference. Why else do you think I suggested these—sterile terms for our marriage? I was trying to show some kind of consideration—to spare you, but now I wonder if I was right.' His hand cupped her chin, making her look up at him. He studied her for a long moment, then released her, his hands going instead to the buttons on his shirt. He said softly, 'Shall we end this farce, *carinha*? Shall we turn pretence into reality?' He pulled off his shirt and tossed it on to the bed. 'Shall we take that shower together and see where it leads us?'

Abby knew exactly where it would lead—to that bed, and a fulfilment beyond her wildest dreams in the arms of the man she loved. For a moment temptation gripped her painfully, then she remembered how one-sided the arrangement would be...

She said almost inaudibly, 'Without love?'

The dark face tautened as he began to unfasten the belt of his pants. 'Is that really so essential?' he asked quietly. 'If you allowed me, Abigail, I think I could give you pleasure.'

'Because you feel sorry for me?' she asked bitterly. 'Thanks, but no, thanks. Pity isn't a motive I care for.'

'And have you no pity for me?' he demanded harshly. He took two strides towards her, pulling her violently into his arms.

As his mouth possessed hers, Abby had to force herself to remain passive. But it was not easy. She wanted to respond to the ruthless pressure of the firm lips exploring her own. The warmth of his skin burned through her thin dress; the stark male scent of him filled her mouth and nostrils.

At long last Vasco lifted his head and looked down into her eyes. 'Why not, *querida*?' he whispered, the intensity in his voice and eyes almost undermining her resolve.

'Because I don't belong here,' she said, making frantic efforts to free herself. 'We don't belong to each other, in spite of what happened back in London.'

'This could be a beginning.' His voice sounded almost sombre. His hand lifted, cradling one small pointed breast in his palm, while his caressing thumb sought the hardening peak through the clinging fabric.

'No!' Abby pushed at him with clenched fists. 'You—you accused me once of allowing Della to use me. Aren't you trying to use me too—in a different way?'

He let her go, his expression bleak. 'I thought we might have used each other.'

'A matter of mutual convenience?' Abby hurled at him, hurting too much to choose her words with consideration. 'No, thank you! I don't want anything else to regret when I walk out of here in six months' time.'

'You are so sure you'll be leaving.' Vasco smiled without humour. 'Perhaps I should make sure that you remain. A baby each year should keep you tied and docile under my roof, don't you think?'

Sudden tears stung her eyes. 'That—isn't even funny!'

'It was not intended as a joke,' he told her grimly. 'I have worked hard, *minha esposa*, these past years to turn this plantation into a paying concern, so that I could afford the kind of life I wanted. Do you know what I saw for myself—a wife, *querida*, children, and a normal family life.' He gave a brief derisive laugh. 'And what have I got? An empty bargain. A half year's agreement, leading to—nothing.' His gaze lashed her, then he turned away, unzipping his pants. 'Now get out. And if you are wise, do not let me find you flirting with Link Dalton or any other of my neighbours in future. No other man is going to enjoy what I am denied, *compreendes*?'

Abby said indistinctly, 'Understood.' And fled.

As the days at Riocho Negro became a week, Abby found time hanging heavy on her hands. A kind of armed truce existed between Vasco and herself, when she saw him at all. He had always left for work before she awoke, and often did not return before evening, and she knew this was through deliberate choice, not necessity, by the obvious bewilderment of the servants.

When he joined her for dinner he treated her with impeccable politeness, but she could not deny there were lengthening silences between them. Personal topics were, naturally, taboo, and she didn't know enough about his work to ask intelligent questions about the crop and its progress. She had abandoned her original intention to ask him to show her round the estate, and she was reluctant to wander round alone, gleaning what information she could, in case she got in the way.

In consequence she found she was retiring to bed earlier each night, and getting up later each day, although such deliberate inactivity was foreign to her nature. She hadn't been able to visualise the kind of life she would be leading at Riocho Negro, but she had not expected to feel quite so isolated and useless.

She had ventured once, in his absence, into the room Vasco used as an office, wondered if there was any typing or book-keeping she could assist with, if only to justify her existence at the *fazenda*, but after a couple of hours poring over what records and files she could decipher, and studying the mass of posters and charts on the walls, she had to admit defeat. He seemed perfectly well organised without any help from her.

And there were months of this—blankness in front of her, she thought bleakly. How could she bear it?

She was trying one morning to interest herself desultorily in one of the paperback novels she had brought with her, when Ana put her head round the door to signal with much eye-rolling that Senhora Gonzaga had arrived.

Abby got reluctantly to her feet, wishing she could feel more enthusiastic about her visitor, and wishing too that she had chosen something more soignée to wear than a simple denim skirt and a white cotton shirt, knotted at the midriff.

She was aware that not one inexpensive detail of her appearance had been lost on Luisa, as she swept smilingly into the room.

'*Bom dia*. I hope I am not intruding. I know but too well how busy one's life is when one is the mistress of a plantation,' she greeted her hostess effusively, just as if she hadn't realised Abby had been spending the morning with her feet up.

Abby smiled weakly in return, and turned to the still-hovering Ana with a stumbling request for coffee.

'A little practice, and you will soon have mastered our language.' Luisa sank into a chair and crossed her legs. Today she was wearing an immaculately tailored pants suit, and the gloss on her boots would have put any mirror to shame. 'So—how are you settling in? I need not ask, of course, if married life agrees with you. You look radiant.'

Her words were so patently insincere that Abby could have laughed out loud.

'Vasco is not here?' The question was casually put, but Abby was not deceived.

She shrugged slightly. 'He's somewhere on the plantation,' she returned. 'Did you want to speak to him about anything in particular? Perhaps I could pass on a message.'

Luisa gave a light laugh. 'Ah no, Dona Abigail, my message is for you. I am merely surprised not to find Vasco at your side, when you have been married such a short time. I hope he is not neglecting you.'

Abby examined a fleck on one of her nails. 'By no means,' she said neutrally. 'Being newly married doesn't automatically require us to spend every minute together. We both—value our independence.'

'You seem to carry your desire for independence to extreme lengths.' Luisa was still smiling, but there was a sting in her words. 'You must understand, Dona Abigail, that servants gossip abominably, and your cook is a cousin of one of my maids. One's private life tends to be public knowledge.'

Abby swallowed. She knew what Luisa was hinting at. No doubt the news that she and Vasco did not share a bed had been a nine days' wonder in this backwater. She managed to keep her voice level. 'Then it's fortunate we have nothing to hide.'

She was thankful when Ana came bustling in with the coffee tray, giving her a chance to compose herself, while Luisa made a few conventional remarks about the weather, and the level of humidity.

By the time Abby had poured the coffee, and they were alone again, Luisa had apparently decided not to probe any further. Not that she had to, Abby thought glumly. Simply knowing that she knew was quite enough. But was that the message she'd mentioned, or was there more?

It seemed there was. Luisa, it seemed, was planning a party early in the following week.

'I hope you will forgive the short notice,' she was saying, as she sipped her coffee. 'Also the lack of a formal invitation. It was a decision made on the spur of the moment, as you say. They are often the most enjoyable, I find, don't you?'

Abby could think of several impulsive decisions she had made which she bitterly regretted, but she smiled and murmured something appropriate.

'So you and Vasco will be able to attend?' pursued Luisa. 'You have no other plans for that evening?'

Other plans? Abby asked herself dazedly. Was Luisa crazy? She spoke as if theatres, night clubs and restaurants were only a car ride away.

She could always say, 'Why, yes. I'm planning to sit and count the minutes until I can decently excuse myself, and go to my room, just as I do every night.'

Instead she said, 'No, a party would be marvellous. We're delighted to accept.'

'That is good.' Luisa set her cup back on the tray, smiling with satisfaction. 'Vasco cannot keep you to himself for ever,' she added lightly. 'It is time you met some people. When my husband was alive the parties at Laracoca were famous, I assure you.' She shrugged. 'I have allowed my widowhood to make me a little lazy, so it is good for me to have an excuse for a celebration.'

It would be good for her too, Abby thought after Luisa had finally taken her departure. It would probably be a very small party—the population in this wilderness was too scattered for anything else— but it would be something to look forward to, in spite of her misgivings about Luisa herself. Something that might rouse her from this lethargy which seemed to be afflicting her these days.

She got to her feet determinedly. And for a start, she would go and find Vasco and convey Luisa's invitation to him. At last she had a genuine excuse to explore the plantation.

She went down the veranda steps, with a word of greeting for Don Afonso who was preening himself morosely, and set off towards the buildings she knew were the drying sheds, although they were not in use at the moment.

It was very hot, the sun beating down relentlessly on her head, and she hesitated for a moment, wondering whether she should have brought a hat. Then she gave a mental shrug. She would soon be in the shade of the plantation.

She was passing a row of houses now, their roofs thatched with broad, thick leaves. Children played between the cooking fires and lines of washing, and women leaned in the shadowed doorways.

They seemed startled to see her, she thought, hearing the rising buzz of voices. Perhaps they had been as little aware of her existence as she had been of theirs, although common sense should have told her that Agnello and the other workers would have wives and families who had to be accommodated somewhere.

But they seemed more upset than excited at her unexpected appearance. Several of them were following her, chattering and gesturing anxiously, and one caught at her arm, pointing back towards the house, as if warning her to return there.

Abby freed herself politely. They probably thought she was lost. She said slowly and clearly, 'Senhor Don Vasco,' and pantomimed the fact that she was looking for him.

But that didn't alleviate their worries at all. Frowns deepened, and heads wagged, and courteously but firmly Abby found she was being urged back towards the house.

My God, she thought, half seriously, is there some ancient taboo about women visiting the plantation? Is it a curse, as it used to be on board ship? Well, I don't believe in such curses.

She squared her shoulders and lengthened her stride with unquestionable determination until she had shaken off her unwanted well-wishers, and within two hundred yards found herself in the shelter of the trees.

CHAPTER SIX

SUDDENLY she was in a different world. She was surrounded by walls of greenery, shaded by an unbroken canopy of leaves. It was very still.

Abby paused a moment to catch her breath. She had the unnerving impression that the forest was holding its breath too, and that unseen eyes were waiting for her to make some kind of move.

And she was tempted to turn and run back to the haven of the *fazenda*.

Idiot! she told herself silently. Fool! She walked forward, realising as she did so that she was not enclosed by untamed wilderness after all. She was in an avenue which had been cleared of undergrowth, and where neatly staked bushes were protected by taller trees. As she walked, her feet sank into a thick carpet of decaying leaves and husks.

The plantation, she saw, was laid out on a rough grid pattern, the jungle being made to conform with the demands of the industry it nurtured.

One avenue gave way to another. Abby trod carefully, listening for some sound of working humanity, but the silence persisted. She turned right and plunged deeper into the plantation, glancing over her shoulder as she did so. She had already walked a long way, and although she'd been counting the number of avenues she had traversed on one hand, and the number of right-hand turns she had made on the other, she still wasn't altogether sure she could find her way back to the *fazenda*.

Perhaps she wouldn't, she thought. Perhaps she would wander in ever-increasing circles for all eternity, or until her bones joined this appalling mulch she was treading in.

She would see cocoa bushes with their strange fan-shaped leaf formations in her dreams, she thought restlessly. The trees in this part of the plantation were much taller and sturdier, but they didn't seem to be fruiting. Not that she would recognise a cocoa bean in its natural state if one dropped on her head, Abby thought bitterly.

She was beginning to wish she'd listened to reason and stayed with the other women, waiting for their men to return. She sighed. Except, of course, that Vasco wasn't her man, and never would be. In fact, if she never came out of this forest, there would be no one to mourn her.

She stopped in her tracks, appalled at the maudlin direction of her thoughts.

'Oh, come on,' she castigated herself. 'What's the matter with you?'

Her energy seemed to be deserting her, and she was aware of the odd lassitude which had afflicted her for the past few days settling on her again, which was not what she needed at all.

She began to walk more briskly, lifting her chin and pursing her lips in a defiant whistle. It was tuneless, but it was infinitely preferable to the silence.

She was so intent on keeping her courage up that she didn't notice the man who had stepped out of the trees in front of her until she had almost cannoned into him.

He was tough and unshaven and carrying a machete, and Abby's whistle turned into a strangled scream. Then she realised he was looking just as startled as she was herself, and she took a firm grip on herself.

She said clearly, *'O patrão?'*

He gaped at her, shaking his head, then broke into an excited gabble, of which Abby understood not a word. Then he stuck the machete into his belt and took a purposeful stride towards her.

This time there was nothing strangled about Abby's scream. It emerged at full throttle as she recoiled, twisting her ankle in the process.

It was as if she'd given a signal. There were men coming from all sides, encircling her as she subsided on to the rotting vegetation, her hand clutching her ankle. And among them, to her infinite relief, she recognised the horrified face of Agnello.

'Senhora Dona Abigail!' His voice was almost a wail as he pushed his way to her side.

Abby tried to say she was all right really, but her voice wouldn't work properly. Her lips moved, but no sound came out, and then the circle of men, still staring at her as if she was some kind of apparition, fell apart, and Vasco was there, his expression a mixture of incredulity and fury as he looked down at her.

He demanded, his voice molten with temper, 'What are you doing here? In the name of God, Abigail, are you quite insane, or is there some explanation?'

'I was looking for you.' It sounded as lame as she was, as he lifted her ungently to her feet. 'Ouch!' She hopped on her good leg, testing the painful one gingerly.

Vasco said something quiet and pungent in Portuguese. The audience was beginning to melt away as silently as it arrived, until only Agnello remained. And he was going too, under the impetus of some order Vasco flung at him, so that they were alone.

She was aware that her twisted ankle had put her at a disadvantage, but she lifted her chin.

'I don't see what all the fuss is about. This isn't forbidden territory, is it?'

'The fuss concerns the way you are dressed.' Contemptuously Vasco indicated her brief denim skirt and slender bare legs. 'Your clothing, or lack of it.'

Abby was totally taken aback. Anyone would think she was indecent! she thought angrily.

She said, 'What's wrong with my clothes?'

'Nothing—for a stroll in an English garden.' His tone was derisive. 'But the plantation does not, alas, fit into that secure category, Abigail, as I thought you would have known. It is part of a jungle, and jungle creatures still inhabit it. Snakes, *querida*,' he added grimly. 'And insects whose sting is poisonous. If you wish to walk here, you wear trousers always, tucked into tall boots. Otherwise, remain in the house.'

Her voice shook. 'Well, as I haven't any boots, I suppose that's the only option open to me.'

He shot her an impatient look. 'You have several pairs, as you would know if you had ever examined the contents of the wardrobe in your room. But you seem determined to live out of the suitcase you brought with you,' he added bitingly.

'Is that any real surprise?' Abby gave him a defiant look. 'Or did you really think I'd want to wear another woman's rejects?'

His brows snapped together in the frown she had come to dread.

'What are you saying?'

'I'm saying I won't wear Della's clothes, or her boots either. Apart from the—the morality of it, they wouldn't fit me.'

There was an ominous silence, then Vasco said, too gently, 'You think—you really think I would insult you like that? *Deus*, Abigail, how dare you make such an accusation! If you had taken the trouble to glance at the clothes waiting for you, you would have seen they are in your size, which I checked while we were in London. If you have some objection to the materials, or the styles—that I could understand. But to assume without evidence that I expected you to accept a gift bought for Della—that is beyond belief!'

Abby's lips parted in a soundless gasp. 'You—bought them for me? But how could you have done?'

'It is not really so difficult.' His voice was grim. 'The wife of a friend of mine has a boutique in Manaus. I telephoned her, gave her a list of what I thought you would need, and described your colouring. When you never used anything Elisa had sent, I presumed you did not care for her choice. It never occurred to me that there could be any other reason.'

'Then I'm sorry I misunderstood.' Abby bit her lip. 'But I'd still rather not wear the things. It's like—charity.'

'Charity?' Vasco echoed incredulously. 'You are my wife, Abigail, so how can it be charity?' He paused, the dark brows flicking upwards. 'Or are you afraid, perhaps, that if you permit me to dress you, I shall also expect to—undress you?'

Colour flared in her face. 'That never occurred to me.'

He sent her a coolly mocking look. 'Then perhaps it should have done. Or do you think I shall be content to live this half-life of ours indefinitely?'

'Six months is hardly an indefinite period,' said Abby, staring rigidly past him.

'You are so sure that such a limit will be set,' Vasco commented drily. There was a silence. 'Do you know yet if you are bearing my child?'

Her flush deepened. 'Not yet—in a few days, perhaps...' Her voice tailed away. 'I'm not—I've never been—very regular, I'm afraid...'

It seemed impossible that she could be standing in a clearing in the middle of Amazonia discussing her most intimate self with a man who was still little more than a stranger to her.

In a way, they had been closer when he was engaged to Della, she thought unhappily. At least then she had been able to take part in a conversation with him without undue awkwardness or embarrassment, secure in the knowledge that her love for him was her secret alone.

Now, one brief, shattering experience had set them at a distance—created an unbridgeable gulf between them.

'So you did not seek me out to tell me you would soon be free of me for ever,' he observed. 'What then did you want?'

'Oh!' Abby's hand flew to her mouth. 'Senhora Gonzaga called to ask us to a party next week—on Wednesday evening. I accepted provisionally. I hope that was right.'

'Wednesday,' Vasco said meditatively. 'I see. Well, why not, *carinha*? Social invitations are few enough in our part of the world, and it is time you saw some new faces, perhaps.'

She thought, If you loved me, I wouldn't need parties, or any kind of social whirl. I'd be satisfied with that alone.

As it was, Vasco must be praying that a few moments of casual self-indulgence on his part wasn't going to result in a life sentence of marriage to a woman he didn't want.

And what am I praying for? she wondered painfully. I don't think I even know any more. If I have to stay here with him, I'm going to be wretched, but if I leave, how can I live knowing I'll never see him again?

Vasco said, 'If you write a note of acceptance to Luisa, I'll see it is delivered.' He glanced down. 'How is your foot?'

It was nothing compared to the deeper ache within her. She said, 'I think it's better, thank you. I'll be getting back.'

'No,' he said, 'you will ride back in the jeep. I have sent Agnello to fetch it. I mean what I say, Abigail. You do not stroll in the plantation without wearing adequate protection.'

'It was your men I needed protection from,' she said huskily. 'They were all carrying those hideous knives.'

His mouth curled. 'Not one of them would harm a hair of your head. They carry knives because we began harvesting the mid-year crop today.'

'Oh.' Abby glanced around her. 'It doesn't look as if there's going to be much of a harvest.'

'These are still young trees,' he said patiently. 'One does not expect too much in the first years of maturity. In the section where we are working, it is very different. It is a good crop, and the main harvest will be even better.'

'No wonder you like it here,' she remarked. 'It's a very peaceful life, isn't it?'

'Do you think so?' His tone was dry. 'Do not be deceived, *querida*. The cocoa bean is one of the most vulnerable crops in the world. Whole books have been written on the pests which attack it, the diseases which destroy it. Raising the bushes to harvest is a gamble always. I have had my fair share of disasters since I came to Riocho Negro.'

She thought, And this marriage—you and I—is just another one for you to bear. Almost inaudibly, she said, 'I'm sorry.'

He frowned, as if he had guessed the tenor of her thoughts. He said, 'Abigail...' then broke off, as the noise of the approaching jeep filled the air. He swore softly, then said, 'At the end of this avenue there is a track which we use to get back to the *fazenda*. Can you walk that far, or do you wish me to help you?'

'I can manage.' Her ankle wasn't hurting nearly as much, but she would have crawled to the jeep on her knees over broken glass rather than experience the bitter paradise of having his arm around her, or having to rely on his assistance in any way.

She said sedately, 'I'm sorry to have interrupted your work, and caused such an uproar. It won't happen again.'

His smile was brief and wintry. 'Not in the same way at least, *faz favor*.' He paused. 'But if you wish to learn about the plantation, then...'

Abby shook her head. 'I don't think so. It's hardly worth it when I shall be here such a short time.'

She began to walk away in the direction he had indicated to where Agnello waited with the jeep. As she went, she found herself wondering whether Vasco was still there, watching her.

Don't look round, she told herself. Don't look round. But in the end, as she reached the track, she couldn't resist a swift glance over her shoulder.

But the avenue was deserted. Only the silence remained.

Abby looked at the dress, and the dress looked back at her.

The trouble was, it was just so lovely. The loveliest thing she had ever had to wear—or not wear, she amended hastily. Because she still totally disagreed with the principle of Vasco buying her clothes, and the fact that she had nothing in her own part of the wardrobe even remotely suitable for Luisa's party should not make the slightest difference.

But it does, she wailed inwardly. Oh God, it does. Who wanted to turn up in a chain store cotton, when there was mist-green silk chiffon, shot with silver threads, crying out to be worn, and wispy silver sandals too which would add inches to her height, and perhaps make her look slightly less insignificant than usual.

Whoever this unknown Elisa was, she certainly knew about clothes, and Abby hoped her boutique was the most enormous success. She had obviously gone to endless trouble to assemble what amounted to a trousseau for Vasco's bride, and it seemed little short of rank ingratitude to go on ignoring all the lovely clothes wilting unworn on their hangers.

She felt the glide of the fabric under her fingers as she touched it tentatively—and imagined how it would feel on her skin.

And she had very little time left; she had heard Vasco go into his dressing-room ages before. She took a nervous look at her watch. She could hardly go to the party in her bathrobe.

She sighed, and gave the alternative dress a look of hostility it did not altogether deserve. Parties in London had been so simple. The only ones she went to were those given by her aunt and uncle, and no one looked at her anyway. She could have gone to most of them with her head in a bag, but this one was proving fraught with all kinds of difficulties.

The servants' attitude was hard to fathom, to begin with. Abby would have thought they would have been glad of an evening's leisure, yet all day she had been subjected to reproachful glances and martyred sighs.

Abby bit her lip. She was going to have to learn some basic Portuguese somehow, even if Vasco was too busy with the harvest to help her. She had tackled him about Ana and the others, but he had merely shrugged, and helped himself to a drink.

She undid her bathrobe and tossed it over the bed, then, fumbling a little, she unfastened the brief lacy bra, and discarded that too. The green chiffon dress left one shoulder entirely bare, so the minimum of underclothes was called for.

'I'll despise myself in the morning,' she told herself, as she carefully lowered the shimmering folds over her newly washed and gleaming hair. 'But tonight I'm going to look like Vasco's wife, not some poor relation!'

She applied some finishing touches to her make-up, then stood back and viewed herself critically.

She felt as if she was looking at a stranger. Abigail, everyone's handmaiden, had vanished completely. Tonight she looked like the favourite concubine instead, the misty glitter of the chiffon paying tribute to her slender curves in ways she had never dreamed possible. She had used eye-shadow, liner and blusher with a steady hand too.

I'm all eyes and cheekbones, she thought with satisfaction, disregarding the fact that no amount of gloss could do away with the wistful curve which beset her mouth.

The dress had its own cape, so she flung it round her shoulders and picked up her bag. As she did so, there was a knock on the door, and Vasco said, 'Are you ready? May I come in?'

Since that first day he had scrupulously avoided intruding on her, using the other door from the passage to gain access to his own room.

Abby turned shyly to face him, as he entered, her heart skipping a beat as she registered once more the unnerving power of his attraction. Tonight he looked magnificent in evening clothes, the white tuxedo complementing his broad shoulders.

She waited hopefully, breathlessly, for some comment from him about her appearance—even some reference to the fact that she had had second thoughts about wearing the clothes of his providing, but all he said was, 'We should be leaving, Abigail. The roads are poor, as you know, and it would be uncivil to Luisa to be late.'

They weren't travelling in the jeep tonight, to her relief, but in a car which had appeared, as if by magic, comfortably upholstered, and fully air-conditioned.

The journey to Laracoca was a lengthy one, and accomplished mainly in silence. Vasco drove

steadily, his brooding concentration apparently
fixed on the vagaries of the road, braking occasionally to avoid some animal which was crossing
their path, and had become dazzled by their
headlights.

It was foolish to indulge in might-have-beens, and
she knew it, but Abby couldn't help wondering what
this drive through the darkness would have been
like if they had been truly lovers. The silence
between them then would have been one of intimacy. When two people were attuned to each
other, often there was no need for words, she
thought sadly. And there would be the possibility
of a baby, a sweet secret for them to gloat over,
instead of a bone of contention.

She smothered a sigh, and rallied her flagging
spirits. After all, she was going to a party, for
heaven's sake, even if she didn't particularly like
the woman who was giving it. And if her physical
estrangement from Vasco was a matter of gossip
among the neighbours, then she would have to do
her damnedest to play the part of the radiant bride,
and convince them all they were wrong to believe
in rumours.

You used to like going to the theatre, she told
herself derisively. Well, tonight you're centre
stage . . .

Certainly at first sight Laracoca might have been
a stage set. Light poured from every window in the
rambling single-storey building, and lanterns were
strung along the broad veranda, and in the encircling trees. A number of cars and vehicles were
parked, to Abby's amazement, destroying her sup-
position that only a handful of people would make
the effort to attend.

Luisa was waiting to greet them, resplendent in taffeta the colour of peonies, her brother-in-law Gerulito beside her. He was considerably her junior, and wore a vaguely resentful air.

'So here you are at last!' Luisa included Abby briefly in her smile, before linking her arm possessively through Vasco's. 'Gerulito, take Dona Abigail and get her a drink. She looks as if she could need one.'

It took all Abby's fortitude to keep her own smile pinned in place. All the years of enduring snide comments from Della and her mother were standing her in better stead than she realised, she thought, as she calmly accepted Gerulito's awkward offer to escort her into the house.

The interior of Laracoca was a revelation. Luisa had clearly spared neither time nor money on creating a luxurious environment for herself. But however lavish the furnishings, the overall effect was hardly homelike, Abby thought as she waited for Gerulito to bring her a glass of fruit punch.

When he returned, she said, 'This is a charming house.'

He shrugged. 'It is adequate. Too many rooms have been added without thought over the years to render it harmonious.'

Abby recalled that he'd wanted to be an architect. She said, 'Well, you'd know more about that than I would.'

'Yes.' His mouth curled peevishly. 'But such knowledge is no longer of any use to me.'

Abby sipped her punch, trying to think of some way to distract him from his grievance. She said, 'I suppose you're harvesting your beans. I hope it's a good crop.'

'The *temperão*?' He shrugged. 'I suppose so. We have a manager, an American, who sees to all that for us. The plantation was João's life, but it is not mine. And I cannot sell it without Luisa's agreement.' He pursed his lips. 'Perhaps she will consent now that ...' He stopped abruptly.

'Now that ...?' Abby prompted.

His sallow skin had flushed. '*Desculpe*. It is of no importance.' He looked deeply embarrassed.

'You mean now that Vasco is married,' she suggested coolly, and he squirmed.

'Forgive me, Dona Abigail. I spoke without thought. It is just ...' He paused again.

'Just that it would have been convenient from all points of view,' she supplied, then relented. 'If you sell the plantation, will you go back to São Paulo?'

It was the right question. His face lit up, and his stilted English relaxed into a broken mixture of Portuguese as he told her enthusiastically about the firm he had been working for, about the projects he had been engaged on. He was clearly even more of a fish out of water in Amazonia than she was, Abby thought, a certain sympathy for Gerulito welling up inside her.

Out of the corner of her eye she saw Luisa sweep into the room, still holding on to Vasco, and found herself wondering why he hadn't waited the customary decent interval and proposed to her. Perhaps he had intended to—only on his vacation he had met Della and fallen madly in love with her, so that nothing else seemed to matter.

And if I hadn't interfered, she thought painfully, he would have broken off their engagement, returned here, and in the fullness of time he and Luisa would probably have got together. Those few mo-

ments of madness in London had spoiled so many
lives, she thought wretchedly.

'Hey, this is a party, not a wake!' Link Dalton
appeared at her side. He gave her glass a disparag-
ing look. 'No wonder you're miserable! Let me get
you some real liquor.'

'No—really, this is fine.' She caught at his arm.
'I'm no drinker. I know the harm alcohol can do.'

He shrugged elaborately. 'Well, don't we all?' He
looked around him. 'Some shindig, huh? Anything
Rio has to offer, the Black Widow can top.'

'I had no idea it would be like this,' Abby confessed. 'Where have all these people come from?'

'You'd be surprised. Those couples over there
have flown in, and are staying a couple of days. A
few come from the settlement. That's the local
doctor, Jorge Arupa. Have you met him?'

'I haven't met anyone really,' Abby confessed.
She paused. 'Except your boss.'

'So I noticed. He was actually smiling, so I
guessed he was telling you about the good old days
back in São Paulo.'

There was an edge of contempt in his voice, and
she looked at him gravely.

'It can't be easy for him, having to adjust to this
life.'

'He doesn't want to adjust, he just wants out.'
Link ran a hand through his hair. 'We just don't
operate on the same wavelength, I guess. I'm into
trees, making them grow strong and healthy, and
he wants to put up concrete tower blocks.' He gave
her a rueful look. 'If they decide to build a new
Brasilia right here, he'll be in his element!'

He paused. 'But let me introduce you around a
little. After all, everyone wants to meet the bride.'

Abby had been aware of inquisitive glances being cast in her direction, so she allowed Link to lead her round the room. Link's laconic tones presenting her as the Senhora Dona Abigail da Carvalho seemed to bring it home to her at last that, however unwanted, she was Vasco's wife. And she was glad that she'd taken such trouble with her appearance. She couldn't compete with the sheer flamboyance of Luisa's style, but it was balm to her spirit to see the admiration in the men's eyes, and the surprised approval of the scattering of women in the room.

'Welcome to Riocho Negro, Dona Abigail.' It was Dr Arupa now, taking over from Link. He was a tall, bluff-looking man with a curling black beard, and he smiled at her with intense kindness. 'Now that you have come among us, perhaps some of our other bachelors will be persuaded to follow Vasco's example. How do you find our climate?'

She began to answer, then paused, aware of a stir of activity at the other end of the room, where long tables bore a bewilderingly lavish assortment of buffet food. Two servants were wheeling in a trolley bearing a cake, alight with candles. There was laughter and applause, and Abby had no difficulty in realising who was the centre of all the attention. It was Vasco, his gaze meeting hers across the room with smiling wryness.

And the significance of the party burst on her full force when the guests began singing lustily to the unmistakable tune of 'Happy Birthday to You'.

Abby wanted nothing more than for the ground to open up and swallow her. It was Vasco's birthday, and she hadn't even guessed! She could understand why the servants at the *fazenda* had

been so put out now. They'd been expecting a celebration of their own.

Her smile felt as if it had been nailed there. Oh,
why hadn't Vasco said something—given some
hint? Luisa was presenting him with a box tied up
with ribbons, whereas she, who was supposed to
be married to him, hadn't even wished him many
happy returns! It brought home to her quite poign-
antly just how much of an outsider she was.

'It is generous of you to share Vasco with us on
such a personal occasion, Dona Abigail.' Luisa's
voice reached her mellifluously. 'Have you already
given him your gift, or do you wish to make your
presentation now?'

Everyone was smiling, looking at Abby expect-
antly, but she was looking back at Luisa, seeing the
mocking challenge in her eyes.

She knows, she thought numbly. She knows I
hadn't the least idea it was his birthday, and she's
going to let me stand here with egg on my face, so
that everyone else knows too.

Vasco said calmly, 'You are quite right, my dear
Luisa. Abigail has already made me a gift.' He
walked across the room to Abigail, took her hand,
and lifted it to his lips. 'The most precious gift a
wife can make to her husband,' he added, smiling
down into her eyes.

There was a burst of laughter, and some clearly
ribald remarks from a few masculine voices.

Luisa's brows rose. 'But how romantic,' she said.
'Are we permitted to know the nature of this gift?'

Vasco's arm slid round Abby's rigid waist,
drawing her against him. 'You must forgive me.
Some secrets are too intimate to be shared, even
with one's friends.'

Abby stared at the floor, feeling the hot colour riot into her cheeks. She supposed she should be grateful to him, for offering an explanation that even Luisa would not dare to question, but how could she be when he'd let them think that—that... She didn't even want to consider what they might be thinking, she thought in an agony of embarrassment.

Vasco had quashed the rumours about their marriage stone dead once and for all. After tonight, no one would believe that they weren't involved in a passionate love affair.

She thought desolately, Only I know the truth, and I'm going to have to live with it.

CHAPTER SEVEN

THE EVENING seemed endless. Abby hoped that after supper they would leave. After all, everyone at the party had a full working day tomorrow, with the usual early start, or so she presumed. But no one seemed in the slightest hurry to depart, least of all Vasco.

And after supper, some of the Laracoca estate workers appeared on the veranda, formed into a makeshift band, and there was dancing, Abby finding herself claimed by one partner after another. She had never been in such demand.

But I won't let it go to my head, she told herself in self-derision. If I had a hump and a squint, they'd still be queueing up to dance with me. I'm a novelty, that's all.

She had also made an enemy. She had looked up at one point in the evening to find Luisa's eyes fixed on her so inimically that she had felt her whole body shrink.

Just be patient, she thought as she turned away. In a few months I'll be gone. You'd have found Della a much tougher nut to crack. She could imagine only too well Luisa's fury and frustration when the news of Vasco's impending marriage had reached her. But the course the marriage seemed to be taking must have given her fresh hope—until tonight.

She still couldn't understand what had possessed Vasco to say such things. In the circumstances, she would have thought him more inclined to give credence to any gossip that the marriage was drifting, in difficulties already, so that the ultimate break would seem readily believable.

She supposed his masculine pride couldn't allow that, and that was why he had behaved so outrageously. And he'd played up to his remarks ever since, to her increasing discomfort, insisting she share with him that first slice of birthday cake, lifting his glass to her in a silent toast whenever he managed to catch her eye, watching her, as she danced past him, as if he could not bear to let her out of his sight.

And all because he can't bear people to think he isn't the great lover, sweeping his bride off her feet, she thought stormily, rejecting the discomfiting memory of her reactions on the sole occasion when he had swept her into his arms.

She didn't want to dance any more, or try and converse with people who spoke at best a smattering of English. Dr Arupa was clearly an excellent linguist, but it was obvious he was already viewing Abby as a future recipient of his services as an obstetrician, so she was trying to avoid him.

As soon as it was possible, she slipped away from the party on the pretext of looking for a bathroom. And she didn't hurry back. The rest of the house betrayed the same love of opulence as the *sala de estar*. Yet it hardly seemed appropriate here in the back of beyond. It was a showplace, but apart from these occasional parties there was no one to show it to.

'Want a guided tour?' Link appeared suddenly in the passage beside her, making her jump.

'No.' Abby hesitated. 'I'm sorry, I must seem horribly nosy.'

'Not at all.' He shrugged. 'It's all here to be looked at. I often look at it myself,' he added drily. 'Just adding up what it's cost the plantation in the past year.' He saw Abby's surprised look, and shook his head. 'No, lady, it wasn't always like this. When Senhor Gonzaga was alive, he made sure the plantation profits were ploughed back into the land. He and Vasco were instrumental in getting government money put into the infrastructure round here, and hell-bent on improving the size and quality of their crop. It was a pity João didn't live to see his dream come true.' He paused. 'On the other hand, maybe it's a good thing he can't see what his grieving widow and his brother have been doing to the place. Every handwoven rug, every imported lamp and silk curtain represents some cut-back— workers fired because they're not prepared to meet the wages bill, the pruning programme halved, equipment allowed to rot away. Need I go on?' He took her arm. 'Come in here a moment.'

It was a small, cramped room, reduced even more in size by the large littered desk, and filing cabinets spilling their contents.

Link walked to a cupboard and extracted a bottle and two glasses. He poured two measures and handed her one. 'Bourbon,' he said succinctly. 'You look as if you could use it, and I know I could.'

It made Abby gasp a little, but as some of it went down she could feel it warming her, removing some of the desolation inside her.

She looked round, recognising some of the charts and posters on the wall as those she had already studied in the office back at the *fazenda*. They carried large illustrations of various insects, as well as cacao leaves suffering from different forms of blight.

Link followed her gaze. 'Depressing, aren't they? And most of them alive and flourishing right here at Laracoca. João had ordered new spraying equipment just before he died. Gerulito's first act as his heir was to cancel it. I've been limping by on what I can scrounge from our neighbours—your own husband included.' He sighed. 'But it isn't enough. At least one hectare is badly affected by *largatão* already, and there could be more.'

'*Largatão?*' Abby frowned. 'I've never heard of it.'

'It's one of the worst diseases a plantation can get,' Link said grimly. 'They also call it *vassoura de bruxa*—witch's broom to you.'

'Witch's broom.' Abby frowned. She remembered Vasco talking about that—the catastrophic effect it had had on his cousin's life. She asked, 'Why is it called that?'

Link shrugged. 'I guess because the diseased shoots are long and distorted, like a witch's talons.' He gave her a wry look. 'It's a romantic notion, I grant you, but there's nothing fairytale about the real thing. Once it gets a hold, it can cost a fortune and some heartbreak to get rid of. Boy, can it spread!' He shook his head. 'I've been telling Gerulito, we should go through that whole area with a fine-tooth comb, but he doesn't want to know.'

In her secret heart Abby felt a little sorry for Gerulito, who was so clearly unfitted to cope with his new role.

'Perhaps Vasco could talk to him,' she suggested.

'Hell, no!' Link said explosively. 'As our closest neighbour, he's the last guy I want to be involved. He's put a lot of investment into Riocho Negro lately, and he won't want to hear about witch's

broom so near his territory. Hopefully, I can deal
with it, and it won't cost him even a night's sleep.'

Abby craned her neck to look at the posters.
'Which one is it?'

'It's here.' Link took her hand and guided it to
the appropriate illustration.

Abby stared at the picture. It looked quite innocuous, she thought, like the kind of misshapen
twig or shoot any shrub might bear, yet it was a
wrecker—a destroyer of lives, even. And she
shivered.

From the doorway, Vasco said glacially, '*Desculpe*. I hope I am not intruding, but I came to tell
Abigail it is time we were leaving.'

'Sure.' Link didn't seem discomposed. 'I was just
filling her in on some of the finer points of the cacao
industry. She's a quick learner.'

'I am sure she found it fascinating.' Vasco's smile
did not reach his eyes. He produced Abby's cape.
'Are you ready, *querida*? Luisa is waiting to take
leave of you.'

All during Luisa's fulsome and prolonged fare-
wells, Abby was aware of Vasco's eyes on her, the
cold, angry set of his mouth.

He did not speak as they got into the car and he
started the engine. They had travelled a fair distance before he said, 'I have spoken to you before
about seeking Link Dalton's company, Abigail.
May I know why you are so determined to defy
me?'

'I haven't defied you,' she protested.

'Then why do I find you alone with him in the
estate office, having deliberately left the party?'

'I'd been to the bathroom. I just—ran into him
in the passage,' she said, despising herself for the
defensiveness in her tone.

'And went with him to the office.'

'Yes, I did.' She sent him a muted glare. 'It's hardly a—a boudoir, after all. And—and at least he talks to me—explains things. We're both outsiders here, and he—understands that.'

'You feel so isolated?' There was surprise in his voice. 'I did not realise...'

'Why should you?' she said fiercely. 'After all, you have your full and busy life, just as you had before I came here. You don't spend all day and every day with nothing to do, except wonder what the servants are gossiping about next.'

'And what is that supposed to mean?'

'Nothing.' Her cheeks warmed slightly.

'I see.' There was a silence. 'And what aspect of cacao cultivation was Dalton discussing with you?'

Her lips parted to tell him, and closed again, as she remembered Link's warning.

'I don't remember,' she said stiltedly, and he laughed harshly.

'So, if it was not the conversation you found so enthralling, it must have been your companion.'

'Oh, don't be so ridiculous—and such a dog in the manger!' Abby flung at him. 'At least Link treats me as if I was a human being.'

'Which I clearly do not,' he said too politely. *'Muito obrigado, senhora.'*

There was no way she could explain to him, Abby thought achingly, as the curt silence descended between them again. There were so many things between Vasco and herself that could not be discussed, that had to remain unsaid, because of the pitfalls which existed in even the most ordinary avenues of conversation.

And, she had to admit, he had offered to teach her about the plantation. It was her own fault she hadn't accepted that particular overture.

But no one could possibly take exception to the kind of innocuous exchange she had enjoyed with Link tonight. Unless Brazilian men were pathologically possessive about their womenfolk, she thought with a smothered sigh.

When they arrived back at the *fazenda*, Abby went straight to her room. She sat down at the dressing table and began to remove her make-up with fastidious care. Without it, she looked far more her ordinary self, she decided, studying the results judiciously. More like a sparrow than tonight's bird of paradise, and no cause for any husband's concern.

She picked up her brush and began to smooth it rhythmically over her hair, but the movement failed in its usual calming effect. The evening had left her on edge, and more than a little forlorn. Vasco was surprised that she felt an outsider, she thought angrily, when he couldn't even be bothered to tell her it was his birthday!

When the door opened suddenly, and he walked into the room and came up behind her, she forgot to be surprised, and glared at him in the mirror.

The arrogant brows rose. 'So now it is your turn to be cross with me,' he observed. 'May I know why?'

'Need you ask?' she demanded stormily. 'How old were you today, Vasco? Or is that a closely kept secret too?'

'I am thirty-three.' He studied her quizzically. 'Is that why you're upset—because I didn't mention that it was my birthday?'

'Is it so surprising?' Abby shook her head. 'It must have been apparent to everyone at that damned party tonight that I was the only one without a clue about what was happening. You should have warned me.'

He shrugged. 'I didn't want to impose the obligation of a celebration on you, *querida*. And the fact that Luisa had chosen this particular date for her party might have been a coincidence.'

'But it wasn't.'

'No,' he admitted. 'It was not.'

'And the servants are upset,' she went on, brushing her hair so fiercely that her head began to ache. 'That never occurred to you, I suppose— or that I might have wanted to give you a present.'

'What did you have in mind?' In the mirror his eyes, dark and curiously intent, met hers, and Abby tore her gaze away.

'I don't know,' she said hurriedly. 'I'd have thought of something—if I'd been given the chance.'

'Allow me to help.' Vasco leaned forward and took the ill-used hairbrush from her hand, placing it gently on the dressing-table.

He said gently, 'Shall I tell you what gift I want from you, *carinha*?' The dark head bent, and he brushed his lips softly along the curve of her bared shoulder. 'I want you, Abigail. Let me stay with you tonight.'

Her heart began to thud, painfully and unevenly. She said, past some constriction in her throat. 'You—you let everyone tonight think that you did so already. Isn't that enough for your pride?'

'Who speaks of pride?' he asked softly.

'I think you do.' Abigail bit her lip hard as Vasco's fingers began to stroke the nape of her neck, slowly and sensuously. 'It—needles you that I seem to prefer another man's company to yours, so you're asserting yourself, proving a point.'

There was a silence, and the caressing fingers stilled momentarily. 'And if that is true?' he said at last. 'Do you think I have no reason? Look at yourself, *senhora*.' His hand cupped her chin, making her meet his gaze fully once again. 'The night we spent together has left no mark on you. You look—untouched, *querida*, a quality that would intrigue any man, and your admirer is very ready to be intrigued, I think. So—I shall remove temptation from his way. From now on there will be no doubt in anyone's mind whether you belong to me or not.'

'There's no need for this.' Her voice sounded strained, desperate.

'And what, *minha esposa* do you know of need?' Vasco mocked. His hands moved, covering her small breasts, and a pang of wild, shameful excitement pierced her body. 'You are my wife, Abigail, but for tonight—be my woman. Forget all this nonsense about love, and remember only that you wanted me once.' His mouth caressed the side of her throat—teased her earlobe. He whispered, 'I hurt you that night, *querida*, and I have never forgiven myself for that. This time there will be no pain, I swear to you.'

No pain, Abby thought with a stunned incredulity. How could he say there would be no pain when he had just dismissed her love for him—the only gift she could give—so negligently? Did he really think he could—use her as a convenient sexual release without making her suffer until the end of her days?

Already, the touch of his mouth on her skin was tearing her apart with longing. Her breasts were swelling under his questing fingers, the nipples already sensitised and erect. A warm trembling had begun to pulsate deep inside her.

It would be so easy to turn to him, she thought dazedly, to offer her mouth, and by implication, her body too. So easy and yet so utterly impossible.

'Relax, *carinha.*' There was cynicism in his smile as if he'd gauged her inner struggle and was weighing it against her involuntary physical re-action to his mouth and hands. 'Don't ask for the moon. When second-best is all there is, why not settle for that?'

Second-best. The words seemed to sear into her mind. All she would ever—could ever-be to him—a shadowy substitute for Della's provocative, glowing beauty.

She thought, I can't . . .

She tore herself free. 'Let go of me, Vasco! I'm not—some parcel that you can unwrap when it suits you!'

Vasco's head lifted sharply, and he stared at her, very pale suddenly under his tan.

He said harshly, 'You don't think so?'

His hands clamped under her armpits, pulling her with bewildering swiftness to her feet. He reached for the zip at the back of her dress, dragging at it so violently that she felt the surrounding threads rip and give way.

She said imploringly, 'No. . .' but it was already too late. The lovely dress lay ruined in a misty green pool at her feet.

He lifted her from it and carried her to the bed, pulling back the covers and depositing her, not altogether gently, against the pillows. Then he bent over her, the powerful hands ridding her almost negligently of her last remaining covering.

Abby cried out and tried to snatch the sheet across her body, but he forestalled her, capturing both her slender wrists in one hand and holding them above her head while he looked at her, the dark eyes ruthlessly assessing every inch of her trembling body.

He said, half to himself, 'I had almost forgotten...'

Sick with humiliation, she closed her eyes. She couldn't bear to read in his expression the comparisons he was bound to be making.

When he released her wrists she hoped for a moment, absurdly, that he had changed his mind. But a swift glance under her lashes revealed that her respite was only temporary. Dry-mouthed, she realised he was taking off his clothes.

She felt the mattress dip under the weight of his body as he came to lie beside her. His fingers lightly stroked the curve of her face, then cupped her chin, making her face him.

He said quietly, 'You're so fragile, *carinha*, like some small, wild bird. It makes me almost afraid...' A faint smile twisted his mouth as he looked into her eyes. 'Almost,' he murmured. 'Yet—not quite.'

His head came down, and his mouth covered hers. Abby felt her body clench in yearning as Vasco's warm lips persuaded, gently pressured hers apart.

His hand slid the length of her body, slowly and possessively rediscovering her, and every nerve-ending throbbed tremulously in response to the contact. Her mind, every emotion, seemed to be shivering in anticipation as he caressed her.

Oh, God, she thought, it's been such a long time. It's been for ever...

Every lonely, restless night she'd endured since she had arrived at Riocho Negro seemed to be urging her on, to take the pleasure he was offering. That sudden dark flare of anger in him had subsided. He was back in control again, his hands exploring her in undisguised appreciation, his mouth kissing her throat, her shoulders, and the slender length of her arms to her wrist, travelling unhurriedly from one quivering pulse to another.

When his tongue found the slight valley between her breasts, the sensation tore a little moan of need from her throat. His fingers shaped each soft mound in turn, moulding them for his kisses, his lips tugging softly and erotically at each rosy, throbbing peak.

He whispered against her flesh. 'Now tell me you do not want me.'

Even if she had been capable of a denial, the sheer physical evidence of her arousal would have belied her.

His hand had moved down to part her thighs, his fingers stroking slowly, tantalisingly across the moist, silken heat of her, making her burn, making her melt. Keeping her, she began to realise, on some agonising, exquisite knife-edge of delight.

She tried to murmur a protest, but the hazy words were instantly muffled, lost beneath the pressure of his mouth. He was still in control, still the master of the situation, she recognised dimly, instinct telling her that this would only last until she reached whatever pleasurable goal he had set for her.

It was like the rhythm of some strange, secret dance, Abby thought wildly, trying to hang on to sanity, with its advance and retreat, its demand and its aching, teasing withdrawal. Her body felt boneless, the blood in her veins as thick and sweet as honey. She lifted languid hands, letting them drift over his shoulders and down his body, over the lean hips and taut, muscular buttocks, offering of her own accord the intimacies he had once demanded from her.

Vasco lifted his head and looked into her eyes, his mouth shaping swift negation.

'Be still, *querida*,' he told her. He began to place a slow, shattering trail of kisses down her quivering body. He said huskily, 'This time is for you.'

Even so she was totally unprepared for the ultimate sensation of his mouth against her.

'No!' The word was forced from her throat in shock and rejection as she tried unavailingly to push him away.

'*Sim*.' His voice was gentle but inexorable. Abby could feel the outraged tension draining out of her as his lips and tongue took their sensual toll, creating a new, almost terrifying intensity of response.

Every emotion, every nerve was stretched to breaking point. Her slim body was moving of its own volition, twisting helplessly, as she wordlessly pleaded for release.

And just when she thought she could bear no more, she felt a soft, elusive trembling deep inside her. Her body lifted against him, tautened as she focused on it, blind-eyed and lost, her whole being concentrated in astonishment and painful joy, as the trembling deepened, took possession of her in a violent, rhythmic pulsation that threatened to tear her apart.

Delight reached some never-before-scaled peak, and she heard herself cry out. In the same second she was aware of Vasco moving, lifting himself, sheathing himself in her, and clung to him, her nails scoring his shoulders as she experienced the swift, heated thrust of his loins, her body writhing in a new, bewildering abandonment. Her anguished sob was stifled by his mouth as his body shuddered in climax, her arms enfolding him with a kind of desperation as she tried to keep him with her, to make the moment last for all eternity.

But nothing did, she realised a few moments later, as she lay beneath him, her body limp and pliant, feeling her heartbeat steady, her breathing return to something like normal.

Did he know, she wondered, her mind hollow, just what he had done to her—how he had made her feel?

But of course he did, a small inner voice reminded her. He was a sophisticated and experienced man, not a raw boy. He had set out quite cynically to possess her, to subjugate her to his will.

He had spoken of pleasuring her, she thought painfully, but not one word of tenderness, or love. But why should he? He knew that she was in love with him, after all. He probably thought she would be grateful—that in future he could look forward to a willing female body in his arms, even if she wasn't and never would be the woman of his choice.

But he had married her, and she was there, she thought, wincing. That was what it all came down to in the end. The passion he'd coaxed from her with such patience was intended to enhance his own enjoyment of his marital rights, after all.

He had found their original bargain a sterile one, she thought almost detachedly. And she couldn't blame him for that. He was virile, and shatteringly attractive, with a working life that was harsh and demanding. No doubt he considered he was entitled to some relaxation—a convenient sexual release when the mood took him. And if he could engender more than mere passivity from his substitute bride—well, she supposed he would regard that as a bonus.

But the last thing he would want was any avowal of undying devotion from her. *Don't ask for the moon*, he had warned her, after all.

He moved slowly, sinuously. There was faint laughter in his voice, and another note, not so easy to interpret. 'Well, Senhora Dona Abigail, can I hope you will welcome me home at night with a little more enthusiasm in future?'

'I wouldn't count on it,' Abby said raggedly.

Vasco lifted himself swiftly on to an elbow, staring down at her, the dark brows contracting ominously as he saw the tears on her face.

He drew a sharp breath. 'What is this? Why are you crying?'

'Did you expect me to be—clapping my hands for joy?' Abby bit her lip. 'Or maybe you thought I was going to congratulate you. Well, I do. You're a—marvellous lover, as I'm sure you already know. But sex without love, however expert, doesn't mean a thing. It—it's little more than an insult.'

There was a terrible silence, then Vasco said evenly, 'You consider yourself—degraded perhaps by what has happened between us?'

'Yes,' she said rather faintly. 'Yes—I do.'

This time the silence seemed endless. Then he said silkily, 'That is—unfortunate, *senhora*. But comfort yourself with this. Having—unwrapped my gift, I find it is not altogether to my taste, and can quite easily be put aside.' He lifted himself to the side of the bed and swung his legs to the floor, bending to retrieve his scattered clothes. As he straightened, he turned back to the bed, taking the edge of the concealing sheet and stripping it away from her, before subjecting her shrinking body to one long, lingering, comprehensive and contemptuous scrutiny. He said with harsh mockery, '*Boa noite, senhora.* I wish you sweet dreams.'

He walked away from her across the room and disappeared into his dressing-room, slamming the door behind him.

Trembling, Abby turned over, burying her face in the pillow, her hands pressed convulsively over her ears. And knowing, even as she did so, that the echo of that slammed door would reverberate in her mind until the end of time itself.

CHAPTER EIGHT

IT WAS the most wretched night Abby had ever spent. She lay staring into the darkness, hurting, unable to find surcease in sleep, and despising herself for her own vulnerability.

She tried to comfort herself that she had managed to retrieve some part of her self-respect, but failed. The price of her pride had been too high, she thought, flinching from the memory of Vasco's scorn, the dismissive, arrogant gaze travelling over her nakedness.

Eventually, weary beyond further thought, she cried herself into an uneasy sleep.

It was late in the morning when she woke, and the sun was pouring into the room through the open shutters. She opened her eyes slowly and unwillingly, and found Vasco standing beside the bed, watching her.

Colouring painfully, she snatched at the sheet, dragging it almost to her chin, and saw him wince, an answering tinge of red burning along his own cheekbones. Then he sat down on the edge of the bed, distancing himself carefully from any physical contact with her.

He said quietly, 'Abigail, I have come to ask your pardon.' He paused. 'The way I behaved last night—the things I said to you—were quite indefensible.'

She said, almost inaudibly, 'It's all right.'

'How can you say that?' he demanded, a harsher note in his voice. Then he sighed, and looked away from her. 'You were, of course, quite right. I can make no excuses for myself. Not for the first time, I allowed my—need for your body to take precedence over my sense of decency. And to make love without love on both sides brings only shame on both sides. You should not have needed to tell me so, and probably that is why I was so angry.' He gave her a swift, bleak look. 'So I ask you to forgive me—for everything.'

Abby felt as if her heart was being wrenched out of her body.

Oh, please, she thought achingly. Oh, please can't you bring yourself to care for me, even a little bit? I love you so much, Vasco, I'll make it enough. If you could only love me with a fraction of yourself, I'd make it last...

But she said nothing. She lay still, watching her hands gripping the edge of the sheet, the knuckles white with the tension she dared not show.

There was a silence, then he said, 'Things cannot, naturally, continue as they are. We both need to think, to decide what is best for the future.' His mouth tightened. 'I—I have to go to Manaus on business for a day or two. Perhaps, away from each other, from the pressures that life here imposes, we will be able to see the situation with more clarity.' His smile was wintry. 'Maybe even find a way of undoing the damage we have inflicted on each other.'

Her throat felt constricted. 'What—what do you have in mind?'

Vasco shook his head. 'We cannot talk now.' He glanced at his watch. 'Pedro Lazaro is waiting for me at the airstrip.'

No ordinary working gear this morning, she realised, but one of his elegant lightweight suits, coupled with a silk shirt and tie, making the force of his dark good looks even more compelling. Desire uncoiled in her, stretched out like a greedy hand...

He went on, 'Whatever decision we make, Abigail, must be a mutual one, but it is impossible to go on as we are. You understand that, don't you?'

She nodded wordlessly. He reached over and detached one unresisting hand from the sheet, raising her fingers swiftly and courteously to his lips. '*Adeus.*'

At the door he paused, and she felt her heart lift in sudden, absurd hope. He said, 'Pedro brought the mail in with him. There is a letter for you on the desk in the study.' He inclined his head with brief formality, and went out.

For the second time in only a few hours Abby watched a door close behind him, and this time there was a finality about it that chilled her.

She was wrong, after all, she thought. Vasco wasn't ready to settle for second-best either. And she found no consolation in the realisation whatsoever.

It was a long morning. With the absence of the *patrão*, the *fazenda* seemed to relapse into a kind of somnolence. Even Don Afonso seemed withdrawn, receiving Abby's half-hearted blandishments with a tilted head and lofty expression.

She was finishing her lunch on the veranda when Maria appeared, holding a thin blue envelope. 'For you, *senhora*,' she announced with a note of reproach.

'*Obrigada.*' Abby took the envelope from her, noting with bewilderment that the superscription was 'Miss Abigail Westmore' and nothing else. Nor did she recognise the handwriting.

She unfolded the single sheet of airmail paper and saw that it was from Keith. As her eyes flicked over the neat handwriting, she realised her failure to retrieve the letter from Vasco's desk had been a Freudian slip.

It was a prolonged grouse from beginning to end, crammed with phrases like 'clearly, my feelings were unimportant' and 'in spite of the upset you have caused'. She had to read it twice before she could decipher the real meaning which was, apparently, that Keith was prepared, albeit grudgingly, to have her back, 'when you've come to your senses', as he put it.

He'd wasted no time in writing the marriage off as a disaster, she thought bitterly. Yet when she had broken the news of it to him in London, he had hardly said a word, just stared at her in ever-increasing outrage. He didn't even have the grace to address the envelope in her married name. In fact, she realised, he hadn't addressed it at all. So how in the world had it got here?

She swallowed. The answer to that was simple. It had been enclosed in a letter from someone else. Someone who knew where she was to be found, and all about Riocho Negro. Someone who also knew Keith.

Abby's mouth was dry suddenly. She drank some coffee, and grimaced at its bitterness.

There could be another explanation, she told herself desperately. Vasco's cousin at the Embassy, for instance. But she was already up on her feet and moving inside the house, and down the hall to the study.

Maria was just starting on the cleaning, but she acceded amiably enough to her young mistress's halting request to come back later.

When she was alone, Abby fell on her knees beside the waste basket, rooting through its contents with shaking hands. What she was doing was foul, despicable, and she knew it, but it made no difference.

She was looking for another blue envelope. It was crumpled in a ball nearly at the bottom of the basket, as if it had been deliberately buried there. She put it down on the strip of carpet beside the desk and smoothed it out. Della's writing, large, flowing, heavily underlined, and quite unmistakable, stared up at her. The envelope was empty, and there was no sign anywhere of its contents. Abby didn't know whether to be sorry or relieved.

She got stiffly to her feet, still clutching the envelope. So Della had written to Vasco. It didn't necessarily mean anything, she tried to tell herself. Perhaps it was just more recriminations—all the things Della had wanted to say in London to his face.

But today the letter had come—and today Vasco had taken the plane to Manaus, without one word of prior warning.

She caught at the edge of the desk, a sudden dizziness assailing her, feeling at the same time nausea rising in her throat.

'Com licença?' Maria peered round the door and gave a startled cry. *'O, senhora!'*

With amazing presence of mind she snatched a clean polishing cloth from her pocket and pressed it to Abby's white lips, before urging her down the passage to the bedroom.

Bending over the basin, Abby vomited until the world tilted and slid round her, vaguely aware of the servants anxiously watching from the doorway.

She said distinctly and politely in English, 'I'm quite all right, really. I've just had a shock.' Then the floor lifted to meet her, and she slid quietly in to an all-enveloping darkness.

'There was no need for you to call at the clinic, Dona Abigail,' Dr Arupa said kindly. 'Had you sent a message, I would have attended you at the *fazenda*.'

Abby flushed. 'Oh, I had to come into the settlement today,' she said with less than truth. 'And I didn't want to cause you unnecessary bother. I'm sure that there's nothing really the matter with me—that it's all quite trivial—something I ate, perhaps,' she added lamely.

Dr Arupa laughed. 'No, Dona Abigail. I suspect you know what the matter is as well as I do.' He gave her a cheerful wink. 'At Dona Luisa's party the other evening, I looked at you and thought, "Soon that little one will be paying me a visit."'

Abby's flush deepened. 'Is it that obvious already?' she asked with an effort.

'Only to the trained eye,' he reassured her. 'What does Vasco say? No doubt he is delighted.'

Abby's throat felt tight. 'He doesn't—know yet.' Her hands gripped together in her lap. 'He's in Manaus. He's been there for nearly a week.' She bit her lip. 'Well, four days, actually.'

He frowned slightly. 'It is a pity you did not come to me sooner, then you could have accompanied him. A friend of mine is an obstetrician there. He could have examined you, carried out some routine tests for anaemia, and so on.' He grinned at her. 'Vasco is my friend, after all. I want to ensure him a happy wife, and a healthy child.'

'Yes, of course.' Abby's answering smile was pallid.

Dr Arupa gave her a searching glance, tapping on the desk with his pen. 'Something concerns you?' he asked quietly. 'You have some inner worry about pregnancy, perhaps, or the birth itself? You have heard, no doubt, about Dona Beatriz, and you are afraid the same thing could happen.' He shook his head. 'Relax, *senhora*, and bloom. Allow yourself to be cherished, and obey the orders of those who have your well-being at heart. But don't become an invalid. Eat the kind of food that appeals to you, and rest when you feel tired. Thus Nature will take its course.'

He made it sound so simple, Abby thought, as she edged her way through the crowded outer room of the clinic. Above the chatter and the noise of crying babies, she could hear the steady thud of rain falling on the corrugated iron roof. An Amerindian girl standing near the door shifted awkwardly to let Abby pass. She was heavily pregnant, her body swollen and unwieldy under the shabby print dress, but as Abby smiled at her and murmured a word of thanks, her grin would have lit up the world.

Abby knew where she would live—in one of those ramshackle houses on stilts rising out of the Riocho Negro itself. Her husband might be one of the lucky ones who earned enough to ensure his family got enough to eat, or he might not, but it seemed obvious from the serene glow about the girl that the coming baby was loved and wanted already.

Abby paused outside the door, fastening her waterproof cape more securely and pulling the hood over her hair against the continuous downpour which had already turned the muddy street of the settlement into a slow-moving orange river.

It had rained every day since Vasco left, adding to Abby's feeling of oppression and isolation, alone at the *fazenda*. And every day he stayed away she became more frightened, more convinced that his absence had something to do with Della.

Abby knew her cousin too well to imagine Della would let a simple little thing like a marriage ceremony stand between her and anyone she wanted. And although her tactics might have shocked Vasco, and embittered him too, it was clear he still cared about her, Abby thought painfully. His attitude to herself after they had made love, his obvious regrets, had revealed that. She had thought she would die of humiliation when she realised Della had spitefully told him about her love for him, but what she'd suffered then was nothing compared with the wretchedness of knowing her love for him would never be enough to draw them together.

She shivered as she stepped out on to the rough planking walkway, shoulders hunched against the rain. She had told Agnello to wait for her near the general store. She didn't even want him to know she'd been anywhere near Dr Arupa's clinic. The servants had been giving her hopeful, sideways glances ever since that stupid fainting fit, and she didn't want to fuel their speculation any further.

The only reason Vasco had married her was to give his child a name, but there was no future for them together, particularly if Della was back on the scene.

And if I tell him that there isn't going to be a baby, then he's bound to let me go, she thought achingly.

Besides, she wanted to be the one who walked away. She didn't want Vasco and Della deciding what was best for her, then breaking the news. And if Vasco thought he could be happy with Della after all, then she wasn't going to stand in his way.

If I hadn't meddled, none of this would have happened, she thought drearily. So the least I can do is disappear discreetly.

The thought of what she was going back to face nearly made her quail. She had no job in England, no home, and would soon have the unenviable status of a one-parent family. She had no illusions about the difficulties of the situation she was creating for herself. But it would be even harder to stay at Riocho Negro as an eternal 'second-best', maintained out of Vasco's sense of duty.

And I'll have his baby, she reminded herself, a part of him to cherish always.

'Hi, there!' A hand descended on her arm, and Link Dalton smiled down into her surprised face. 'You sure picked a great day for it—whatever it is?' he added on a note of enquiry.

Abby shrugged evasively. 'Just some—shopping. I was getting tired of staring at the same four walls. I fancied a change of scene.'

'Well, you got that all right,' Link conceded. He took her arm and began to pilot her along the walkway. 'Why didn't you get a message over to Laracoca, and then we could have come in together, like I suggested that time?'

Abby bit her lip. 'Oh, it was a spur-of-the-moment thing.'

'OK,' he said easily. 'Well, we're both here now, so why don't we live a little—take the town apart? Have a drink, see that film show I mentioned?'

Abby hung back. 'Agnello's waiting to take me back...'

'Back to the same four walls,' he reminded her. 'Let him go. I'll bring you back myself later.' He grinned at her. 'Come on, *senhora*, relax—enjoy yourself. When I spotted you just now, you looked wetter than the rain!' His tone didn't alter. 'Vasco still in the big city?'

'Yes,' she said, and forced a smile. 'Well—perhaps it could be fun.'

But Agnello's expression when Link revealed their plans told a very different story. His brows shot up in shocked disapproval and he burst into a flood of excited Portuguese. Abby had no idea what he was saying, but the looks which he was spiking in her direction needed no interpretation.

She touched Link's arm. 'Maybe this isn't such a good idea, after all.'

'Oh, don't take any notice of Agnello. Some of these Brazilians are more hidebound than the Pilgrim Fathers,' said Link with a trace of impatience. 'I thought English girls were supposed to be liberated. Besides,' he added with odd deliberation, 'you can bet whatever Vasco's been doing in Manaus, he won't have been attending any church services.'

'No.' Her throat felt tight suddenly. She turned to the little man. '*Calma*, Agnello, *esta bem*.'

The expression on his face indicated that it was far from all right, but he made no further attempt to dissuade her, merely lifting both clenched fists towards the waterlogged sky before climbing into the jeep and heading off.

Abby and Link were left facing each other.

'I feel almost daring,' she said. 'Isn't that absurd?'

'If it makes you smile, it isn't absurd at all.' He paused. 'I think the first item on the schedule is a beer. There are two bars, a respectable one, and a dive. Unfortunately to get to the respectable one we have to ford this river they call a street.'

'Then let's make it the dive.' Abby forced herself to sound cheerful.

He laughed.

'Right on, lady, but don't say I didn't warn you!'

They should have braved the mud, Abby realised immediately, but to start carping about her surroundings would only make her sound foolish, so she sat down at the stained table Link indicated. The beer which emerged from a dilapidated refrigerator was cool and refreshing, although she had serious doubts about the glass it was served in.

Link said ironically, 'Not quite the setting for the Senhora Dona Abigail, wife of the lordly *fazendeiro*.'

There was a note in his voice that irked her. She said quietly, 'Please don't refer to my husband like that.'

'I'm sorry.' He looked repentant. 'I guess I can't get used to the fact that you're really married to the guy.'

Nor me, Abby thought bitterly, but she remained silent.

'Another no-go area, huh?' Link raised his hands in mock surrender. 'But you can't blame me for wondering. Everyone likes a mystery.'

Abby drank some beer. 'I don't see what's so mysterious about two people getting married,' she returned composedly.

'No.' His eyes remained on her face, openly speculative. 'Except there are people around, myself included, who would swear Vasco's *noiva* was called Della. Unless, of course, that's your middle name.'

'No,' she said, 'it isn't.' She kept her voice steady. 'I think there's been some confusion somewhere along the line.'

'Well, the name came from Vasco himself, so he must be the one who's confused,' said Link drily. 'Perhaps it's one of the penalties for falling in love.'

'Don't you have first-hand experience?' Abby tried to steer the conversation into safer channels.

'No,' he said. 'I've always moved around too much, I guess. It's not easy to form a commitment to someone when you don't know where you'll be the next week, let alone the next year.'

'But you're settled here, aren't you? You have your work...'

'I have a job that's running out fast,' he corrected. 'Gerulito isn't even pretending to take an interest any more. He wants to sell, and go. He was in Manaus a few days ago, trying to fix up a deal, but it didn't work out. The Black Widow nearly hit the roof when he told her,' he added with a reminiscent grin.

'Why did she do that?'

He shrugged. 'Maybe she isn't ready to give up yet.'

Abby touched a drop of moisture on the outside of her glass. 'Laracoca is a beautiful house.'

'It's that all right,' he agreed. 'But I wasn't talking about Laracoca. It's your husband she wants, *senhora*, or she did. Maybe after the big row she had with Gerulito, she'll cut her losses and go back to São Paulo. She's not the kind who'll stand in line for a man. She likes to call the shots.'

Abby thought of Luisa's forceful, triumphant beauty, and felt a little sick. 'I'm sure she does.' There had been a note in Link's voice which had puzzled her, and she gave him an uncertain look. 'Does that upset you?'

'It's not my place to be upset,' he said shortly. 'I'm the hired hand, and she's never let me forget it—not for a minute. Well, I don't stand in line either.'

Her brows drew together. 'I'm sorry.'

'Don't be,' he said. 'I have no illusions. I never did.' He gave her a considering look. 'Life can be easier to take that way, Senhora Dona Abigail. Maybe you should let a few of your illusions go too.'

'I don't think I have that many.' Abby took another look around the bar, her feeling of unease deepening as she encountered the glances of the two girls sitting at the bar who were the only other women there. They were garishly dressed and crudely made up, and beneath the cosmetics their expressions were not friendly.

She pushed her glass away. 'I think I've out-stayed my welcome here.'

Link followed her glance, groaning slightly. 'I'm sorry, I really shouldn't have brought you here, but in a place this size there isn't that much choice. Come on, and we'll get something to eat.'

When they went outside Abby found the rain had stopped at last, although the wind was blowing in swift, warm gusts. Link took her to a street stall sheltered by a makeshift awning where a plump woman served them bowls of a thick yellow soup tasting of shrimp and garlic.

'*Tacaca,*' Link told her with amusement, seeing the faint apprehension on her face. 'Try it—it's good.'

And after the first tentative mouthful, she discovered it was. As they ate, Link chatted lightly about the places he had visited, and the other work he'd done, but he included few personal details, she realised. He was a loner, certainly. The career he had chosen revealed that. Even if Luisa had been attracted to him, she wondered whether he would have stayed. But then everyone was different, she thought as she scraped out her bowl. Not everyone was like herself, committed to one man come hell or high water, and that was probably a good thing. She banished the thoughts that were beginning to crowd in on her. It was safer and better to think about someone else's problems instead of her own.

She was quite aware she shouldn't be here with him like this. Speculative glances were following every step they took. But that was inevitable when they were so obviously not Brazilians but strangers—outsiders. She found herself wondering what they would have made of Della. What they might still make of Della, she reminded herself painfully.

Using Link's company as a barricade against her own wretchedness clearly wasn't working, and common sense told her that she should scrap any idea of accompanying him to the film show and request, instead, to be taken back to the *fazenda*. But there was nothing for her there except emptiness and loneliness. At least she could keep the inevitability of that at bay for a little while longer.

The film show was an experience in itself. A tin shack, Link had told her, but he had exaggerated. The building consisted of a corrugated roof held up on rickety-looking poles, and the audience sat on benches staring at the elderly screen. Everyone at the settlement seemed to be there, the women on the benches with their children beside them or on their laps, the men lounging at the back smoking. The programme began with a newsreel. In between a lengthy piece about a new hydro-electric plant, and some Middle Eastern troop movements, Abby caught a glimpse of the Princess of Wales looking ravishing. One day, a lifetime ago, she had stood at the front of the crowd to watch the Royal bride pass by, on her way to St Paul's. She thought of London, and the smell of the streets after rain had washed them, so different from the dank, heavy smell from the surrounding forest here. She took a quick, unsteady breath. There were so many things she could not find it easy to forget, and that was the least of them.

The newsreel was followed by a serial, set in the days of the fabulously wealthy rubber industry in the last century, and featuring a heroine whose stupidity and innocence seemed equally impregnable as she resisted the advances of the rich and handsome hero in order to fulfil some vow of entering a convent.

If only it was as simple as that, Abby thought with a sigh.

'Had enough?' asked Link, aware of her sudden restlessness.

'No,' she said. 'We may as well get our money's worth.'

The film was *West Side Story* and it was obviously as familiar to the rest of the audience as it was to herself. She wished it had been a more cheerful offering. As the story moved on to the in-

evitable tragedy at the end, she felt answering tears
sting at her eyelids.

'You're very quiet,' Link observed afterwards as
they walked to the jeep. 'I wanted you to have a
good time.'

'Oh, I did,' she assured him with false brightness.
He smiled. 'Sure.'

There was silence between them as they drove
away from the settlement. Link's attention was
fixed frowningly on the road, and it needed all his
concentration, Abby thought, wincing, as they encountered yet another pothole.

Wearily she made herself relax, allowing her
lashes to droop on to her cheeks. Time seemed to
pass, and she was aware of the jeep slowing,
drawing to a halt. She opened her eyes, sitting up
with a jerk. 'Are we there already?'

But they didn't seem to be anywhere in particular. The jeep's lights were illuminating the road,
and the clustering trees—no lamplit windows or
other sign of habitation.

She looked at Link warily. The evidence seemed
to suggest the unthinkable, but she still couldn't
believe it.

He didn't look back at her. Still gripping the
steering wheel, he said flatly, 'I told you in the bar
the job was running out. I'm not waiting around
for it to happen. I'm leaving, and soon. What I
need to know is—do you want to come with me?'

She gasped. 'Are you crazy?'

'Some of the time, but not now,' he said. 'So
what next? Are you going to tell me you're married?
I know that. Are you going to tell me you're happy?
Because I don't believe it.'

Abby was shaking inside. 'I don't understand any
of this.'

'Yes, you do, honey,' he corrected. 'I'm making you a proposition. We've both lost out in Riocho Negro, so why don't we leave?' He turned and gave her a level look. 'You're not fooling anyone with that marriage of yours, Senhora da Carvalho. Oh, sure, Vasco played the part of the loving husband the other night, but that was because he knew Luisa was doing a number on you.'

She ran her tongue round dry lips. 'Did—Luisa put you up to this? Does she want me to go so she can have Vasco?'

'Hell, no!' He sounded genuinely surprised. 'Since the row with Gerulito, she knows better than that. No, you've intrigued me since that first day, Abby. I've never seen any newly-wed girl look as untouched as you do.'

Colour flared in her face. 'That isn't true...'

'Oh, stop kidding yourself.' Link spoke quite gently. 'You can't keep many secrets round here, and you and Vasco haven't been using the same bedroom since you got here. Add to that the little discrepancy over the names, and we have ourselves quite a story.'

Abby pressed her hands against her burning face. 'Well, please don't waste any sleep over it,' she said angrily. 'I—we're perfectly content...'

'You may be, honey,' he told her drily. 'But I can guarantee Vasco isn't. He's in no all-fired hurry to come back from Manaus, is he now? Don't you want to know why?'

She shook her head wordlessly, terrified of what she was going to hear.

'Abby.' Link reached out a hand and stroked a strand of her soft hair. 'What's the point of sticking your head in the sand? The guy's cheating on you. Gerulito saw him coming out of the best hotel in the city with this dazzling blonde. He couldn't believe it. Most men would be content to bring back one European chick, but two?' Link shook his head.

Abby said through stiff lips, 'You don't know she's European. She could be—be one of those girls...'

'A hooker?' he supplied. He shrugged. 'Maybe, but if so, she travels a long way for her tricks. Gerulito was so fascinated he went into the hotel and asked who she was—spun the clerk some story.' He paused. 'It seems she's a Senhorita Westmore from London—making an indefinite stay.'

CHAPTER NINE

ABBY had once read somewhere that people under sentence of death sometimes welcomed the day of execution, because it finally put an end to their terrible uncertainty. But she didn't believe it.

Because an eternity of doubt would have been easier to bear than knowing that all her fears had become reality, and that Della was here in Brazil, and back in Vasco's life and heart.

If, she thought, wincing, she had ever really been away.

'Does her name mean anything to you?'

She had forgotten the man sitting quietly beside her, as she had fought against the tidal wave of hurt and grief rising inside her.

The muscles in her throat were tight as she swallowed. She said, 'Not a thing. Will—will you take me back to the *fazenda*, please?'

'Right now?' There was a note of incredulity in his voice. 'Aren't you going to give me an answer first?'

'Answer?' she echoed dazedly. How could she answer questions when she was breaking apart inside?

'To my proposition,' said Link on a note of impatience. 'You can't be planning to stay with the guy, Abby. Not now.'

There was a certain truth in what he said, a part of her mind acknowledged numbly. As soon as Vasco returned from Manaus she would tell him she was leaving—spare him the awkwardness of telling her that he wanted her to go.

Link reached over and possessed himself of her hand. 'So why not come with me?' he urged. 'Riocho Negro hasn't been lucky for either of us.' He paused. 'I'd look after you, Abby—show you a good time. And I wouldn't—push you too fast. I'd let you dictate the terms.'

He was attractive, and leaving with him would be a let-out—a salve for her pride, if nothing else.

His fingers were warm against hers, but that was all. There was no *frisson*, no curiosity about the taste of his mouth. She felt empty, drained of all sensation.

She thought, It wouldn't be fair, and realised only when she heard his sharp intake of breath that she'd spoken the thought aloud.

'What's fair about anything in this whole goddam mess?' He let go her hand. 'Don't decide now, Abby. Give yourself a few days. I have some things to finish up at Laracoca. You can get a message to me any time you want.'

But she didn't have a few days, Abby thought, as he re-started the jeep. She needed to make her escape at once. But how? she wondered desperately. This wasn't London with its trains, and Tube, and taxis. She couldn't just—walk out. But she couldn't turn to Link for help. Everything within her shied away from such a solution, even from using him merely as a travelling companion.

It seemed she would have to rely on Vasco, who would be only too glad in the circumstances to help her on her way.

The final degradation, she thought numbly.

They completed the remainder of the journey in silence. Abby was aware of Link's fleeting sideways glance seeking her from time to time, but she made no attempt to respond. She felt too weary, her mind circling on the same dreary treadmill.

When the lights of the *fazenda* finally blazed through the trees she sat up sharply, feeling her heartbeat quicken erratically.

As the jeep pulled to a halt in front of the veranda steps, Link peered forward with a surprised exclamation. 'He's back!'

Abby said thickly, 'Yes.' She opened the passenger door reluctantly and slid to the ground, her eyes fixed on the dark figure lounging with apparent negligence on the veranda.

As she approached the steps, Vasco swung his booted legs down from the table and rose courteously to his feet. He was smiling, but Abby could sense the anger in him, as tangible as a clenched fist.

'Bem-vindo,' he said silkily. 'Welcome home, *carinha.'*

'I—I wasn't expecting to see you.' Abby was aware that Link had come to her side.

'So I gather,' he said pleasantly. 'Good evening, Link. I believe I must thank you for escorting my wife.'

'In your absence,' Link said flatly.

'That is true.' Vasco's mouth curled. 'I shall take care to avoid any more such absences.'

'That sounds a great idea.' Link put his hands on his hips and faced him pugnaciously.

'But we must not keep you,' Vasco went on. 'I am sure you have duties to occupy you at Laracoca, and my wife and I wish to enjoy our reunion.'

'Oh, really?' asked Link. 'Maybe Abby has other ideas about that.' He turned to her. 'What about it? Do you want me to hang around?'

'The decision is not hers to make.' Vasco's tone was still polite, but it held cold finality. 'And, to you, my wife is Senhora da Carvalho. Please remember that.'

'Maybe you're the one who needs to remember——' Link began, but Abby caught at his arm.

'No!' she said urgently and miserably. 'Go, Link, please.'

For a moment he hesitated, his face wearing a frankly goaded expression, then he nodded. 'OK, honey—anything you say.' He lowered his voice. 'But don't forget—all it takes is a message.'

The jeep's engine roared into life, and the vehicle disappeared into the night, leaving husband and wife facing each other in silence.

I'm not standing here as if I've been struck dumb, Abby thought with a sudden flash of anger. She walked forwards up the steps, heading for the front door, but Vasco blocked her way.

'Where are you going?'

'To my room. I'm rather tired.' She stared down at the boards of the veranda, avoiding his gaze.

'Oh, but you cannot run away yet, *querida*.' He spoke lightly enough, but there was an implacable note in his voice. 'It is some time since we saw each other, after all, and we have so much to talk about.' He gestured at the bottle of whisky and glasses which stood on the table. 'You'll have a drink with me? No? Then we'll have a pleasant cup of coffee together.' He clapped his hands sharply, calling to Ana as he did so.

'I don't want to talk now,' Abby said desperately. The moment of confrontation seemed to be upon them, and she couldn't face it. 'Please, Vasco...'

'We could talk in the bedroom if you prefer.' His brows lifted mockingly. 'No?' He pulled a chair forward for her *'Faz favor de sentar-se,'* he added politely.

She was glad to have a seat, because her legs were suddenly shaking under her. She sat stiffly on the cushions, staring into the darkness, silence closing round them again. Out of the corner of her eye she saw Vasco produce a cheroot from a case in his shirt pocket, and the flare of the match as he lit it.

She had rarely seen him smoke, she thought. Perhaps he was ill at ease too, with no more relish for the difficulties of the coming interview than she had.

Ana brought the coffee, setting the tray on the table and almost scuttling away again, her eyes flicking swiftly from one stony face to another.

Vasco waited a moment for Abby to pour the coffee, and when she made no move to do so performed the task himself, handing her a cup with an imperative gesture.

'Drink it,' he said, adding acidly, 'You look as if you need it.'

Abby lifted the cup to her lips, swallowing some of the hot, fragrant brew, managing by some miracle to keep her hand steady, aware that Vasco was watching her.

At last he said softly, 'Well, *minha esposa*? Have you nothing to say to me?'

So many things, she thought desolately. But all of them totally unutterable. He was planning to end her life, to send her back like an unwanted gift, and he was sitting there, drinking coffee with that half-smile playing round his lips.

Anger gusted in her. She wondered crazily what he would do if she flung herself at him, screamed at him, kicked him, bit him, punched him with her fists.

But she couldn't do that. For the sake of what little self-respect she had left, she had to play it cool.

She ran her tongue round her dry lips. 'You— told me to think about our marriage. Well, I have— and I've decided I want to leave you—go back to England.' She drank some more coffee. 'So I'd be glad if you'd make the necessary arrangements for me.'

'How simple you make it sound,' he said, after a long pause. 'Did it escape your attention, *querida*, that I told you any decision must be a mutual one?'

'No.' She put the cup carefully back on the table. 'But it's what we both want, after all. It has to be...'

'*Desculpe*, Abigail, but you are wrong. I have no intention of letting you go.' Vasco's voice was heavily sardonic. 'In fact I have the best reason in the world for keeping you at my side.' There was another silence. 'Well, have you still nothing to say to me?'

Abby was unable to think of a word. She felt stunned, totally bewildered. She looked at him and saw the pleasant, smiling mask had gone. Vasco looked thunderously, murderously angry suddenly. She shook her head.

'Then you will listen,' he said harshly. 'When I returned today, and Agnello came to me and told me you were still at the settlement with Dalton, I decided to come and find you—to bring you back.'

Her head lifted sharply. 'You did that? But why?'

'Isn't it obvious? This is not London, Abigail. Here a married woman does not flaunt herself in public with a man who is not her husband.'

Colour flared heatedly in her face. 'That's the most ridiculous thing I've ever heard!' Her voice was strained and husky. 'And what about married men? I suppose they're allowed to—flaunt themselves with anyone they please, and no one turns a hair.'

'That,' he said grimly, 'is not the point under discussion, *senhora*. The fact is I went to the settlement, and failed to find you. Instead I met my good friend Jorge Arupa.' He paused, then said flatly, 'He was—delighted to see me. I am sure you know why.' He watched her flush deepen hectically, and nodded. 'Exactly.'

'Oh, God,' she whispered. She couldn't have allowed for that, a voice in her head whispered. If she'd known he would be here waiting for her like this, she might have stayed in the jeep with Link, made him drive her away somewhere—anywhere.

'So, where were you?' Vasco's voice bit at her, making her start. 'Why was it so impossible to find you?'

She found a voice from somewhere. 'We went to the film show. And had a drink.'

'A drink.' His brows snapped together. 'Where?'

She tried to remember. 'The—the Olinda, I think . . .'

'Ah,' he said too quietly. 'So he took you there—where the whores go. Perhaps he thought it appropriate.'

Abby made a little sound in her throat, then snatched up her cup and hurled its contents at him. Realising her intention, he dodged, but the coffee still spattered the shoulder and sleeve of his shirt, and he swore furiously.

He gritted between his teeth, 'You necd to be taught a lesson, *senhora*—in manners, if nothing else!'

He took a step towards her, and Abby backed away. 'Don't come near me!' Even in her own ears, her voice sounded thin and nervous.

'And don't tell me what to do,' said Vasco with soft but chilling emphasis. 'You are my wife, Abigail, and you are staying here with me, no matter what plans your lover may have for you.'

'He isn't my lover!' she said on a little wail of protest, because he was still advancing on her, and she was trapped against the veranda rail nowhere left to retreat to.

'Not yet, perhaps,' he corrected icily. 'In fact, not ever. You belong to me, *senhora*, and I think you need to be reminded of that in a way you will never forget.'

He scooped her up into his arms as if she was a child, and holding her against his chest, carried her into the house, accompanied by a series of loud and malevolent squawks from Don Afonso.

'Put me down!' Abby's low voice simmered with rage. 'Let go of me—or I'll scream my head off, and the servants will hear.'

Vasco laughed harshly. 'Scream away,' he advised. 'No one will come to your help. They will think only I am giving you the beating you so richly deserve.'

The arms which held her were like bars of steel, making a nonsense of her struggles. Vasco walked with her into the bedroom, kicking the door shut behind him, before carrying her to the bed and dropping her against the pillows.

Gasping, Abby hurled herself on to her knees and slapped him across the face as hard as she could.

The force of the blow sent a shock up her arm, and left the imprint of her fingers in bruising relief against his bronze skin.

She stayed on her knees, staring up at him, frozen with horror, as she awaited his retaliation.

He said, half to himself, on a note of bitter mockery, 'And I promised myself I would be gentle with you.' His hands closed on the V-neck of her cotton shirt, dragging the edges apart with a kind of considered violence, ripping the buttons from their holes. One swift wrench disposed of the strip of fabric that joined the lacy cups of her bra, and she was bare to the waist.

His hand closed insolently on one small breast, his palm moving in slow, demanding circles against her nipple.

Hardly breathing, Abby said, 'I hate you.'

Vasco shrugged, his other hand sliding down to deal with almost negligent ease with the fastening on her jeans. 'Then what have I to lose?' he asked ironically.

His invasion of her wasn't brutal, but at the same time she was left in no doubt that she was being punished. He showed her none of the heated sensuality which had pervaded their lovemaking on the night of his birthday. Instead he was almost casual, using her body to obtain for himself an insultingly swift gratification. He had not, her numb brain registered, even bothered to remove his clothing.

She lay under him, when it was over, outraged, despoiled—yet even then feeling deep within her the first torment of her own uncurling need. She felt shamed to her very soul.

An eternity passed, then Vasco sighed harshly, lifting himself away from her and propping himself on one elbow while he looked down at her.

He said, 'So you understand me now, do you, Abigail? You believe me when I tell you that you will stay here with me, and bear this child we have made, and our other children. And there will be no more nonsense of closed doors between us either. From now on you share this bed with me.'

She made a little sound, and his mouth curled.

'You find the prospect unappealing? *Que pena!* Irksome as this marriage may be, *carinha*, it exists, and I intend to make it real for both of us.' He paused. 'I promise, however, to try and contain my lusts within acceptable limits. Once a week, perhaps—isn't that the convention?'

Abby flinched from the blatant cynicism in the dark eyes. If the last few minutes was a sample of what she would be asked to endure, she didn't think she could bear it. Not after he'd shown her so devastatingly what passion could be.

She said huskily, 'And what about Della?'

He was very still for a moment, then he said quietly, 'Ah—your letter was obviously an enclosure. I should have realised...' There was a brief pause, then he said, 'She need not concern you. All that can be allowed to matter is our life here together, and the well-being of our child.'

'You can say that?' she managed out of her dry throat. 'You can keep me here, knowing...' She couldn't go on.

'You know why you are here. We settled that in London.' His voice was hard.

'And if there was no baby?' Her eyes were fixed painfully on his unrevealing face. 'Would you let me go then?'

'The question does not arise.' He yawned, stretching. 'And now I am going to take a shower.

Are you going to crown our blissful reunion by taking it with me?'

'No!'

He laughed. 'That is what I thought. However,' his forefinger traced the curve of her hip, 'I could insist, or even—persuade you to change your mind.'

Abby said quietly, 'Haven't you humiliated me enough?'

He lifted a brow. 'You regard the normal intimacies of marriage as humiliating. I shall have to teach you differently, *amada*.' He sat up and began to unbutton his shirt, his voice deepening in mockery. 'But some other time, perhaps. When you are more accustomed—resigned perhaps to our new relationship.'

'You think that can ever happen?' The word 'resigned' made Abby shudder inside.

'I think it will have to, if we are not to spend the rest of our lives in purgatory,' he jibed, stripping off his shirt and dropping it on to the floor, then getting to his feet to rid himself of the rest of his clothes.

Naked, he crossed to the wardrobe, opened one of the massive drawers it contained, and extracted one of Abby's nightgowns. He returned to the bed and let it fall like a drift of thistledown across her body.

'You see how thoughtful I am,' he told her sardonically. 'Hide yourself in that, *querida*. I won't trouble you again this evening. But please don't expect me to be equally modest,' he added, carelessly brushing his knuckles down the curve of her averted face. 'I have never worn pyjamas in my life, and I do not intend to start now.' He paused as if waiting for some reaction from her, and when there was none, he shrugged, and sauntered into the bathroom.

Abby lay very still, staring into space, listening to the distant splash of water. If nothing else, she thought, wincing, she now knew what to expect from him, and the realisation chilled her blood.

Clearly he no longer harboured any scruples about sex without love, she told herself wretchedly as her body burned in frustration. No doubt he considered he was simply being practical in a totally impractical situation. He had married her out of some weird combination of duty and chivalry, and now that he was stuck with her, he was making the best of things, as he saw them.

And there was still Della to consider. Abby wondered if her cousin was in Manaus at this moment in her expensive hotel suite, waiting to hear from Vasco that his unwanted marriage was over, and that they were free to be together.

She could imagine Della's fury on hearing she was to be thwarted yet again. But that didn't necessarily mean the end of the relationship between them, she reminded herself unhappily.

Della had already demonstrated that she was prepared to go to any lengths to get her own way. Perhaps she intended to stay in Brazil, and Abby would have to accustom herself to Vasco's periodic absences to visit her.

She sat up, shivering, and pulled on the nightgown. She couldn't honestly believe that Della would be inclined to stay in Manaus as Vasco's kept woman, living on the sidelines of his life. But then it had never occurred to her that Della would come to Brazil to win him back, either. From the beginning, it seemed, she had underestimated the strength of their feelings for each other.

But perhaps they had underestimated her too, she thought slowly. Whatever Vasco's motives for marrying her, and keeping her with him, the fact remained that she was his wife, and was going to be the mother of his child. Surely she could build on that? At any rate she would try, she promised herself fiercely.

Starting now, perhaps. She slid off the bed, straightening the covers as she did so, and went over to the dressing-table, looking at herself long and hard in its mirror.

She had never worn this nightgown before, or any of the others of Vasco's providing, but she had to admit it was lovely. And she couldn't doubt it had been intended for her alone. The deep apricot shade of its filmy folds warmed her pale skin and contrasted with her brown hair in a way it would never have done with Della's flamboyant blonde beauty. It was enticingly sheer too, but in a subtle way, veiling her slender curves without total concealment.

The shower, she was aware, had stopped. Hastily Abby grabbed up her brush and began to smooth her hair with long rhythmic strokes.

Her hair was curving to her shoulders as sleek and glossy as a bird's wing by the time Vasco came back into the bedroom. He was wearing a towel draped round his hips, and drying his hair on another. Abby watched him in the mirror under her lashes, feeling excitement clench inside her like a fist as she studied the smooth play of muscle in his chest and arms.

Silently she willed him to look at her—to become aware of her regard. She put down the brush with a clatter, and tilted her head back a little, letting her hair swing like a silky curtain. But totally wasted, she realised with a pang of disappointment, because he hadn't even glanced at her. He looked weary, and more than a little preoccupied, she thought, the lines of his cheekbones and jaw more prominent than usual. In spite of his avowed determination to go on with their marriage, he wasn't happy, she thought. But how could he be?

And what the hell did she think she was doing, playing the part of the unwanted seductress?

Vasco was in bed now, arranging his pillows for sleep, his back turned to her, totally oblivious to her pathetic attempt to attract his attention.

Sudden tears stung at her eyelids, but she forced them back, rising and moving like an automaton. She slid under the covers, staying near the edge, heart-stoppingly careful not to intrude on any territory but her own.

It was the first time they had ever shared a bed for the night, but there was no intimacy in it, no sense of mutuality. Abby felt as if she was marooned somewhere on a distant star in a dark and unfriendly universe. She could hear Vasco's steady breathing, but it meant nothing, because even if she stretched out a hand—reached for him, she knew he would not be there for her.

He had not, she thought ridiculously, even wished her 'Goodnight'.

And, with a kind of despair, How am I going to bear it?

CHAPTER TEN

IT WAS very warm, and very humid. Abby sat on the veranda on a cane lounger, fanning herself with a device of plaited leaves which Agnello had made for her.

She had been touched to the heart by his consideration, and had thanked him in her stumbling Portuguese. It was evident that everyone at Riocho Negro knew she was pregnant, and was wishing her well.

It was, she thought drearily, almost the only consolation she had.

The three weeks which had passed since Vasco's return from Manaus had proved to be the most difficult of her life, relations between them so strained, she felt ready to snap.

It was not, she reminded herself hastily, that Vasco was in any way unkind. At times he was almost too considerate, too concerned for her well-being.

And too bloody polite, Abby thought with sudden violence.

It was useless dwelling on yet another round of 'might-have-beens', she knew, but it could all have been so different if he had married her for the right reasons—if their child had been conceived in love. In those circumstances, this waiting time could have been fun, full of warmth and laughter and anticipation. If they had had a normal marriage, she could have grumbled cheerfully about the nausea which seemed to assail her most mornings these days, instead of desperately trying to control it until Vasco had left for the plantation.

But the first time she had attempted an admittedly poor joke about some of the side-effects of her condition, he had looked at her bleakly.

'I am already aware of your resentment of my child in your body,' he said quietly. 'You do not need to emphasise it.' He had left the house before she could find the words to tell him that she hadn't meant that—she hadn't meant that at all.

So now, whenever he asked her how she was feeling, she replied, 'Fine,' even if it wasn't strictly true, like this morning when she'd woken with a backache like a nagging tooth.

She must have slept awkwardly, Abby decided, gently waving her fan. And was it any wonder, when she spent most nights in such a state of abject tension?

Vasco had, she thought, been as good as his word about troubling her as little as possible. And on the few occasions when he had turned to her in the darkness, it had been a swift, perfunctory easing of his physical needs. The passion he had shown her once was no more than a memory, growing more distant and less credible with every night that passed.

And yet, stupidly, she still hoped that one night he would take pity on her, and delight her famished body with the caresses and the fulfilment which she craved from him.

Even though, she thought painfully, his whole attitude revealed his distaste for the necessity of having to make love to her at all, and his wish to get the whole thing over with as quickly as possible.

She sighed, and rubbed her back. She was so starved of contact with him that sometimes, in the mornings, while he was in the bathroom, she would roll across the bed to lie for a few moments in the hollow his body had left, burying her face in his pillow to breathe the scent of his skin.

On one occasion she had actually psyched herself up sufficiently to follow him to the bathroom. 'You once invited me to have a shower with you,' she'd planned to say. 'Well, here I am.'

But the cold astonishment on his face when she had appeared diffidently in the doorway had silenced the carefully rehearsed words on her lips— that, and the way he had silently reached for a towel and fastened it round his waist.

He had spoken mockingly about the 'normal intimacies' of marriage, she thought, but there were none. Except for a few brief, clinical minutes once in a blue moon, he kept her severely at arm's length, mentally as well as physically.

'No more closed doors,' he had said, too. Yet the barriers that separated them now were worse than any locked wooden panel. And she had no idea how to break them down.

Perhaps when the baby was born, things would be better. Vasco wanted an heir for this estate he was maintaining against all odds in the wilderness. If she could give him a son, perhaps this would kindle some affection in him towards her at least. When he returned in the evenings, she wanted the right to go into his arms without the fear of rejection.

She heard the sound of a vehicle and straightened, wondering if Vasco was returning. He had gone to the settlement some time before with one of the workers who had cut himself badly enough to warrant stitches.

But as the jeep came into view, she realised the driver was Link Dalton.

He got out, and walked up the steps.

'I've come to say *adeus*,' he said. There was a pause. 'You never got in touch.'

It was a statement, and a critical one. Abby reddened. 'No.'

'You disappoint me, Senhora da Carvalho.' His tone was heavily ironic. 'I thought you had too much spirit than to allow yourself to be pushed around by a guy who can't stay faithful.'

'Whatever I feel about that,' Abby said steadily, 'it doesn't automatically mean I'm prepared to— throw in my lot with someone who's a comparative stranger to me.'

'Nice point,' he said laconically. 'But I guess a more cynical man might ask himself just how well you knew the great *fazendeiro* when you married him.' He shrugged. 'I suppose I can't blame you. He can offer a more comfortable life-style than I can afford—for now, anyway. And even when this place collapses round him, he has his rich Rio family to bail him out, so you won't starve.'

Abby lifted her chin. 'I think you're confusing him with Gerulito,' she said. 'I can assure you Vasco has no intention of letting Riocho Negro go to pot. The mid-season harvest has been one of the best yet and...'

'And he's hoping for great things from the main crop, and from that vast nursery of seedlings he's sunk his money into.' Link shook his head. 'He'll be lucky to make a dime on it. That's the trouble with expanding in the cocoa bean industry too fast, too soon. You can't be everywhere, especially at harvest time.'

'He works incredibly hard,' Abby protested indignantly, and Link laughed.

'So you can defend him, even after what he's done for you,' he marvelled. 'Well, maybe *o patrão* would have done better to keep away from the drying sheds, and see what's going on elsewhere. Witch's broom isn't exclusive, Senhora Dona Abigail. It travels on the wind up to fifty kilometres, and Laracoca isn't anywhere near that far away.'

'You mean Vasco's cocoa trees could be diseased because there's witch's broom at Laracoca?' Abby got to her feet.

'There's no could be about it,' he said. 'I gave myself the guided tour as a farewell present before I came up to see you, and I'd say eighty per cent of his new trees are affected.'

'But there must be something that can be done.' Abby felt sick, physically shocked.

'Sure there is,' he shrugged. 'You cut away the diseased part, and some over, and you put the whole lot on a big fire, well away from the rest of the plantation. And you take care you get it all, because if you don't, witch's broom just spores again, and you're back to square one.' He shrugged again. 'Alternatively, you do like Gerulito's planning, and you walk away, back to the big city, and leave cocoa growing to Bahia, where they don't have nasty diseases like this.'

He paused. 'Of course in Bahia, they don't have city boys and no-hopers running the industry either.'

'How dare you!' Abby's voice rose furiously. 'What do you know about running an estate when you can just—shelve your responsibilities and move on whenever you feel like it?' She gave an unsteady laugh. 'And you actually thought I'd go with you! I wonder how far along the line you'd have ditched me too.'

'That, lady, is something we'll never know.' There was an unbecoming flush in Link's face. 'But I could have shown you a better time in bed and out of it than your high-toned *senhor*. At least you'd have had my undivided attention—as long as it lasted.'

'I think that counts as a lucky escape,' Abby said shakily but defiantly.

'And I would agree.' Vasco's voice seemed to be compounded from ice and steel.

Abby jumped. She'd been too worked up to notice his silent approach from the direction of the drying sheds.

She said with a gasp, 'Oh—I didn't know you were back...'

'That is evident.' He did not look at her. His eyes were fixed on Link Dalton as he walked up the steps. He said, 'How can I make it clear to you that you are not welcome on my estate?'

Link shrugged. 'I just called round to say goodbye,' he said. 'And to offer your bride a ride out of here. But it seems she prefers to stick around, no matter how many blondes you have holed up in Manaus.'

Vasco's face seemed to have been carved out of granite. He said quietly, 'How good of you, *senhor*, to take such a close personal interest in my private life. Now will you leave, *faz favor*, or do you wish me to throw you down the steps?'

'OK, OK!' Link held up a placatory hand. 'I'm really not into rough stuff.' He gave Vasco a tight unfriendly smile. 'It's a pity you're going to be so short of dough. The Black Widow and her brother-in-law are following me out. They're going back to São Paulo, so Laracoca is up for grabs. You could have bought it for a song—only I guess you won't be doing much singing round here for a while.' He slanted a frankly lascivious grin at Abby. 'So long, doll. Have what fun you can,' he added, and walked down the steps to his jeep.

Vasco's eyes glittered with temper, and some other less easily defined emotion, as he turned them on Abby. 'And what is that supposed to mean?' he demanded dangerously.

She found her voice. 'Vasco, it's *largatão*—witch's broom. Link says it's attacked most of your new young trees.'

He was very white suddenly under his tan. 'Witch's broom?' he repeated on a note of incredulity. 'But how?'

'It's all over Laracoca,' said Link, getting behind the wheel of the jeep. He switched on the engine and leaned out of the window, shouting to make himself heard. 'I told your wife all about it some weeks ago. Maybe she forgot to pass the message on.' He shot Abby a look, partly derisive, partly malicious, and drove off.

Abby stood facing her husband. The look in his eyes was enough to turn her to stone, she thought.

'Is it true?' he asked hoarsely. 'Did you know there was witch's broom at Laracoca, and yet said nothing?'

Slowly, fearfully she nodded, and saw his face twist in pain and rejection.

She hurried into speech. 'It isn't like you think,' she said desperately. 'Link talked about it to me, but he told me to say nothing—not to worry you unnecessarily. He said he'd deal with it . . .'

Her voice trailed away. Vasco stared at her for a long moment in silence, then he closed his eyes as if the sight of her was abhorrent to him.

He said, half to himself, '*Deus*, I did not realise until now how much I had made you hate me. But you have had your full measure of revenge, have you not, *senhora*?'

He turned away and went down the steps two at a time, shouting for Agnello as he went.

Abby watched his flying figure disappear, and a little groan escaped her. She had meant, after the conversation with Link in the Laracoca office, to mention the subject of witch's broom very casually to Vasco, but that had been the night he had made love to her, and that, together with subsequent events, had put everything else out of her mind.

But I should have remembered, she hit at herself. I should have said something to warn him, in spite of Link.

She ran indoors, going straight to her bedroom. She stripped off the blouse and skirt she had been wearing, replacing them with a long-sleeved shirt and a pair of serviceable jeans, and forcing her feet into a pair of the long boots Vasco had once designated.

She was probably making a complete fool of herself, she thought wretchedly, but she needed to help—or at least make the offer, she amended forlornly. The last look Vasco had given her had not suggested any assistance from her would be welcome.

The last time she had gone through the section where the plantation workers lived, there had been a peaceful, even lazy atmosphere. But there was no sign of that today. A pick-up was departing, crammed with most of the younger women and a lot of the older children too.

Abby shouted to the driver to halt, and pelted after it. It lurched to a standstill, and hands reached down to pull her aboard. She was almost too breathless to say, 'Thank you.'

No one else seemed to be saying anything either. They seemed all to have been struck dumb by the unexpected arrival of the *Senhora* among them. On all sides, Abby was encountering looks of wary embarrassment.

She said, 'Oh, please, I want to help,' inwardly cursing the language barrier as she saw their uncomprehending expressions. She tried again, struggling to put words together. '*Quero—ajudar.*'

Again there was silence, and glances were exchanged, then an older woman leaned forward, giving Abby a toothless smile, and proffering a murderous-looking machete.

Abby said, '*Obrigada,*' and meant it. She wasn't one of them, and maybe she never would be, but this was an emergency, so her presence had been accepted.

She found herself wondering if Vasco would be as merciful.

She clung to the side of the pick-up as it lurched through the trees. The other women had begun to sing, a low almost tuneless chant, and Abby found her own body beginning to sway, with theirs, in time to the music.

She found she was looking at her surroundings with a new awareness. There were bananas growing in the gaps between the cocoa trees, she recognised, and some of the other trees used as a shade canopy were familiar too, although she couldn't put a name to them.

She thought, I'll ask Vasco...then paused, wincing. Even if she made reparation for her terrible blunder by fighting the witch's broom at his side, there was no guarantee he would forgive her, or trust her sufficiently to tell her anything about the plantation. She sighed. Instead of hanging about the house, feeling sorry for herself, she should have been down here with him, learning about his work, about the way he provided for her, and the estate workers. Perhaps on that basis alone they could have achieved some kind of rapport, and she could have been some use to him.

At least there would have been something to talk about, she acknowledged painfully. Something to fill those endless impenetrable silences between them.

Because now it was probably too late.

No! She felt the protest so forcefully that for a moment she thought she might have uttered it aloud. It couldn't be too late, no matter what Link might have claimed.

She felt sick when she thought about him. She had genuinely liked him, looked on him as a potential friend, thought she could trust him. So how had it all gone so hideously wrong?

It occurred to her that in spite of his cynical offer to take her away with him, the woman he had really wanted was Luisa, even though he had scornfully described her as the Black Widow. Abby could see now how that might have been a cover-up for much deeper feelings.

Her own dislike of Luisa couldn't alter the fact that she was a beautiful and voluptuous woman. There could have been the burgeoning of an affair between them, Abby thought, except that Luisa wanted Vasco instead, and made no secret of it.

She remembered Link's bitter references to Vasco as 'the great *fazendeiro*', and thought she could understand them now. To Link, Vasco must have seemed the man who had everything—a successful plantation which could afford to support its own workforce, a respected position in the community—and any woman he wanted, including Luisa.

Link must have found that a bitter contrast to his own situation, she realised with reluctant sympathy. She could understand the resentment which must have been festering in him, probably for a longer period than he had realised himself.

And hearing Luisa's hysterical reaction to the news that Vasco was meeting Della in Manaus must have been the final straw in convincing him he was wasting his time over her.

A flock of small birds rose in a noisy cloud in front of the pick-up, startling her out of her uncomfortable reverie. She saw they were entering a section of the plantation that was entirely new to her. There had obviously been a stringent clearing programme before planting, and the tiny trees were staked out with almost mathematical precision.

Abby studied the nearest ones as the pick-up halted and its occupants began to scramble down. The trees looked all right to her untutored eyes. Perhaps the whole scare was an invention on Link's part—a piece of deliberate spite.

She swung herself to the ground and looked round her, wondering if someone would show her what to do. She was totally unused to any kind of cultivation. Her aunt and uncle's house in London had possessed an elegant rear garden, and there had been some land attached to their weekend retreat in Suffolk too, but they had employed gardeners to attend to each of them. Abby had never had so much as a window-box of her own.

She hated the feeling of helplessness her ignorance engendered.

All around her, work had begun. People were moving methodically along the rows of leaves, hacking off the shoots and tossing them into piles behind them.

Squatting to examine the tree nearest to her, Abby could see that some of the shoots seemed to be abnormally elongated and swollen. She remembered the information Link had casually flung at her. *'You cut away the diseased part, and some over...'* Handling the machete gingerly, she cut away the distorted tissue and threw it behind her. But had she got it all? she wondered frantically, peering at the rest of the fan-shaped branches.

A hand touched her shoulder, lightly and tentatively, and she looked up into the solemn brown face of a small boy aged about ten. Silently he pointed at another shoot and nodded. When she had hacked it through and discarded it, he helped her to her feet and led her to the next tree. Amusement mingling with gratitude, Abby realised he had appointed himself her mentor.

She squatted awkwardly, cut where he indicated, and moved on. The singing had died away now. There was only silent, concentrated effort all around her, and she was part of it, part of a pattern, an aching, back-breaking rhythm.

There was sweat dripping from the end of her nose, and trickling between her breasts. The handle of the machete felt slippery in her fingers, and she had to keep wiping her hands on her jeans. The shoots were tougher than they looked too, and her hands were getting sore. She was going to have blisters, but it didn't matter.

I'm such a wimp, she thought in self-derision as she saw how effortlessly the other women seemed to be working. One or two of them even had babies strapped to their backs.

And I would have been spending the morning with my feet up, Abby thought ruefully.

The pain in her back seemed to have subsided, or maybe she just couldn't single it out from all the other aches and twinges which were besetting her. She had left her watch in her bedroom, and all sense of time had deserted her. Only the movement of the sun above the canopy of trees gave her any indication of how the day was passing, that and the sheer weariness of her muscles and limbs.

The boy tugged at her arm. *'Devagar, senhora, devagar.'*

He was telling her to go more slowly, but how could she, when there were still rows upon rows of trees stretching into the distance?

Out of the corner of her eye she saw that everyone seemed to be slackening off. Clearly it was time for some kind of break. Abby's guardian vanished, returning a few minutes later with a shawl which he spread on the ground beneath one of the banana trees, motioning her to sit.

She subsided thankfully, leaning her back against the trunk, and wondering if she would ever have the strength to get up again. She closed her eyes, but opened them at another tentative tap on her shoulder. The boy was holding out a canteen of water.

The water was warm and tasted of chemicals, but it was the best drink she had ever tasted. She could have finished the lot, but she was careful to leave at least half, as she wiped the mouthpiece and handed it back to him, with a smile.

'*Como se chama?*' she asked. 'What is your name?'

He squirmed with pleased embarrassment at her interest.

'Afonso, *senhora*,' he mumbled, and Abby nodded. She wondered if it was a tradition that estate workers should name their children after the *patrão* and his *senhora*. If so, maybe the next generation would throw up a crop of little Vascos and Abigails, she thought idly, liking the idea.

Afonso picked up a broad leaf and began to fan her with it, then stopped abruptly, jumping to his feet. Abby forced her drowsy eyelids open to find Vasco standing staring down at her, his face a grim mask of displeasure.

He said, 'When Agnello told me I did not believe him. Are you quite insane?'

'I don't think so.' The words ended on a gasp as Vasco reached down and jerked her, without gentleness, to her feet. Afonso, she saw, had tactfully disappeared into the undergrowth.

Vasco said, 'You will go back to the *fazenda* immediately, Abigail.'

'Oh, no,' she said, 'I won't. You can shut me out of your life, and your heart, but you can't stop me making amends for all this.' She gesticulated wildly around her.

She must be suffering from heat exhaustion, she thought dazedly, otherwise she would never have dared be so frank. And, later, she would probably regret bitterly that she had allowed him to glimpse, however briefly, the emotional anguish that this non-marriage of theirs was costing her. But now, somehow, she didn't care any more.

She found her voice—that stranger's voice—again. 'I'm your wife, Vasco—the wife of the *patrão* of Riocho Negro, and I have a right to be here. I should have told you about the witch's broom at Laracoca, and I know that now, but I didn't realise how important it might be. But I do now, and you've got to let me do this. I need to do it, damn you—I need it!' There were tears suddenly mixing with the beads of perspiration on her face, and she lifted clenched fists, pummelling violently at his chest. She repeated chokingly, 'I—need this.'

His hands closed over hers, stilling them. He said with sharp authority, '*Calma*, Abby. You don't know what you are saying—what you are doing.'

'Yes, I do. You have to let me help. You owe me that at least.'

'*Querida.*' He hadn't spoken so gently to her for weeks, she realised. 'There is no question of owing. And you have done enough. Go back to the house—*faz favor.*'

'No.' She stared past him at those endless lines of trees, now wavering in the oddest way and the pain in her back had returned stronger than ever, making her whole body tense watchfully. She sank her teeth into the inner softness of her lower lip. 'Oh, what's the use? You don't want me here. You never have. Nothing I do will ever make any difference...'

She was babbling, she realised, because the pain was frightening her now, lashing at her savagely. All that bending and stretching, she thought. She must have pulled a muscle.

Vasco said harshly, 'What nonsense is this?' His voice sharpened. 'Abby—what is it?' His hands were hard, clasping her face.

There was nothing, suddenly, but the pain. Abby looked up into Vasco's face, saw the dark glitter of his eyes, the swift strained lines of his mouth.

There was something, she thought dimly, that she needed to say to him. Some reassurance she needed to give. She was aware her lips were moving, but she couldn't hear what they were saying, because the roaring of blood in her ears was too loud, too overwhelming.

As his arms closed forcefully round her, she cried out, and let the hot, painful darkness take her.

CHAPTER ELEVEN

THE WITCH'S talons were clawing at her, tearing at her flesh, and Abby heard herself whimpering. A voice said gently, '*Calma*, Dona Abigail,' and the pain began, magically, to recede.

When next she opened her eyes the room seemed full of the pungent acrid scent of smoke. She said hazily, 'They're burning the witch...'

A man's figure was standing by the bed. As Abby focused, she saw it was Dr Arupa.

He said, '*Sim, senhora*. They are indeed doing so.' He paused. 'How do you feel?'

'My head swims,' she decided as she tried to sit up. 'And I hurt.' She sank back against the pillows, looking at the doctor's kind, grave face. She said, 'I lost the baby, didn't I?'

'Regretfully, yes, Dona Abigail.' He sat down on the edge of the bed. 'May I know when you first realised something was wrong?'

It seemed a lifetime ago. She said, 'I woke with this pain in my back. But it stopped—for a while.' She sank her teeth into her lower lip. 'If I'd rested, would it have made any difference?'

He shook his head. 'I think not, Dona Abigail. Often these things are inevitable—nature's way.' He gave her a reassuring smile. 'But you will be as good as new in a few days.' He proffered two tablets and a glass of water. 'Now take these, and rest again.'

She swallowed the tablet obediently, and let the world slip away again.

This time, when she woke, Vasco was stretched out in a chair beside the bed. He was grimy and unshaven with lines of strain showing clearly in his face. The faint smile he sent her did not reach his eyes.

He said quietly, 'How are you?'

'Better, I think.' Her lips felt dry, and she moistened then with the tip of her tongue. 'Vasco—I'm sorry...'

'You are not to blame,' he said bleakly. 'Perhaps it is even a blessing in disguise.'

If he had struck her, the shock couldn't have been greater.

But she supposed she should have been expecting it. By losing the baby, she had removed the sole reason for their pathetic excuse of a marriage to continue any longer. And Vasco was signalling without pretence or prevarication that he wanted his freedom.

She said in a muffled voice, 'I—I'm sure you're right, but I can't quite see it like that—not yet. Maybe in a few days...'

'Maybe.' He gave a weary nod of agreement. 'Jorge assures me you are going to be perfectly well again very soon, Abigail.'

There was a silence, then he added politely, 'I hope the smoke does not trouble you too much?'

'Oh, no.' She forced her mouth into a travesty of a smile. 'Do you think you've managed to get rid of it all?'

'We can only hope,' he said. 'I have no means of knowing yet whether the next crop of mature pods will be affected or not. Only then can I truly begin to count the cost.' He got to his feet, grimacing. 'But I must not burden you with my troubles.' He lifted her nerveless hand and brushed it swiftly and meaninglessly with his lips. '*Boa noite*, Abigail.'

She watched the dressing-room door close behind him, then turned over, burying her face convulsively in the pillow. She had thought, for a little while, that the way he had spoken to her in the plantation had bordered on tenderness. But it had just been concern for the baby, after all. Nothing for herself.

And now there was no baby, he wanted to be rid of her and install Della, his real love, in her place.

Looked at objectively, she supposed it was the ideal solution to the entire situation. But she couldn't be objective now that she was actually faced with the reality of being sent away. The ache of emptiness in her body bore no comparison to the wrenching emotional pain she was experiencing.

Couldn't Vasco have spared her for a few days—at least until she was back on her feet again, she thought, her hands balling into small, tight fists. Or did he think it was better to be cruel to be kind, and leave her in no doubt about his plans for the future?

The residue of Dr Arupa's tablets ensured that she slept for at least part of the night. She felt well enough to get up the next day, but Ana would not hear of it. Instead she coaxed Abby into a fresh nightgown, and brushed her hair until it shone, tying it back with a lemon ribbon to match her gown.

Abby found all these refinements unnecessary, and was tempted to say so, but she was glad she hadn't protested, when Ana opened the door a little later and ushered Luisa into the room.

There was an edge to the smile she bestowed on Abby. 'I am so sorry to learn you are indisposed,

Dona Abigail, and the cause. I had no idea...' she added, and paused, looking genuinely embarrassed.

'The grapevine must have broken down,' Abby said quietly. 'It's—kind of you to visit me.'

'I had intended to call anyway, to say goodbye.' Luisa nodded. 'Yes, it is true. Gerulito is returning to the life he is fitted for, and I am going with him. After all,' she added with a sigh, 'there is nothing to keep me here now.'

'Since the death of your husband, of course,' Abby said politely.

She saw Luisa's eyes flicker for a moment, then the other woman gave vent to a little, artificial laugh. 'Of course,' she echoed.

There was another silence, then Luisa asked, 'And you, Dona Abigail, when will you be leaving Riocho Negro?'

So the rumours had begun already, Abby thought grimly. She said, 'Nothing's been actually decided yet.'

'*Noão?*' Luisa paused artistically. 'Yet I understood from Vasco... I must have been mistaken.' She examined her immaculate fingernails. 'But to leave is a sensible decision. You have a saying in England, I think—to flog a dead horse.' She shrugged. 'Why should one wish to?'

'Why indeed?' Abby agreed. 'I presume that's your own conclusion, too.'

There was another loaded pause, then Luisa rose. '*Adeus,* Dona Abigail. We shall not, I think, meet again.' She kissed the tips of her fingers to Abby. 'And accept my condolences once again. Although Vasco must, in the circumstances, be relieved he has not an extra mouth to feed, after all.'

Abby watched her sweep to the door, wishing with all her heart that the laws of hospitality didn't forbid her to fell her parting guest with a water carafe.

It hurt to know that Vasco had even hinted to Luisa that Abby's time at Riocho Negro was strictly limited. But at least he had left Luisa herself in no doubt that she had nothing to hope for from him, and that had to be a slight consolation, thought poor Abby.

The day passed with appalling slowness, punctuated by visits from the servants with little trays of appetising delicacies, including her favourite poached chicken breasts.

They were trying so hard to comfort her for the loss of the baby, Abby realised gratefully. What they didn't yet know, of course, was that she didn't simply have a miscarriage to mourn, but the shattering of her entire life. And she found herself wondering how they would fare under Della's autocracy.

The day passed slowly, and was succeeded by another and gradually the pall of smoke began to lift from Riocho Negro.

Vasco visited her punctiliously morning and evening asking politely and conventionally how she was, to which she would reply brightly and conventionally that she was feeling better all the time.

It wasn't a total lie. Her body was recovering as rapidly from its trauma as Dr Arupa had predicted, and he was delighted with her progress.

'I shall miss my visits here,' he announced one morning, as they drank coffee together on the veranda. 'But I really have no excuse to continue them. It is time you put this setback completely behind you, Doña Abigail, and got on with your life.'

Abby tried to return his smile. 'I still get rather depressed at times.'

'Of course, that is only natural.' He patted her hand. 'But that will pass. What you need is another baby, and as soon as possible, as I have told Vasco.'

Abby swallowed. 'You—did?'

'*Sim,*' he said cordially. 'He was obviously concerned that you should be totally restored to health before...' He paused delicately. 'So I was glad to be able to put his mind at rest.'

She felt as if all her facial muscles had tightened unbearably. Vasco had not, during the past days, given the impression of someone seeking peace of mind. The courtesy he had invariably shown her was only a façade. Beneath it, Abby sensed both wariness and tension in his dealings with her.

She bit her lip. And she could imagine his inner reaction to the doctor's jovial suggestion that they should have another child. He had been sleeping in the dressing-room since the day she had lost the baby, and there had been not the slightest hint that this arrangement would ever be altered while she remained at Riocho Negro.

He was distancing himself, she had come to realise, for the inevitable confrontation.

She waved goodbye to the doctor and came back up the veranda steps. Don Afonso croaked '*Bom dia*' at her, and gave vent to one of his menacing cries. Then for the first time, he flapped his wings and stretched out his neck, indicating that he was prepared to allow Abby to tickle him gently. Usually Vasco was the only person permitted such intimacies.

She sighed. 'Oh, Don Afonso,' she whispered, 'are you making friends with me at last, just when I'm leaving?'

She stared around her as she smoothed his feathers. Vasco's domain, she thought sadly, his little kingdom in which she had never been more than a usurper.

She lifted her head. But she would not be sent packing, she vowed silently. Somehow she would find the strength to walk away, as she had intended, her flags flying and her pride intact.

She was certain none of the servants had been within earshot of the veranda while she had been talking to Dr Arupa, yet dinner that night had embarrassing overtones of celebration. Rosa had added an extra course, and made some deliciously elaborate, tongue-tingling sauce to go with the duck which was the centrepiece of the meal.

In spite of her inner turmoil, Abby found she was eating ravenously. Comfort eating, they called it, she thought, as she sat back, replete, and something she would have to watch when she was alone again, or she would end up like a small barrel.

Afterwards they sat on the veranda, while moths swooped around the lamp on the table. Abby was aware her hand was shaking as she poured the coffee. Vasco had lit another cheroot, which seemed an ominous sign, or was she simply being hysterical? she wondered.

At last he said quietly, 'Abby, I am told by Jorge that you are now well again, so it is time we talked seriously together. We are confronted by a situation which needs some harsh decisions and...'

'And you're going to tell me what you've decided.' Her voice was pitched a little higher than usual.

'No,' he contradicted sharply. 'We need to talk— to think what is best...'

'You said this before,' Abby reminded him, 'before you went to—to Manaus. But when you came back there was no discussion. You—imposed your own solution on us both.' She took a deep, deep breath. 'That—isn't going to happen again, Vasco. I've already decided what I want.'

'Which is?'

'To leave Riocho Negro.' She kept her voice steady by a supreme effort. 'To go back to England.'

'Alone—or to meet your lover?'

For a moment she was silent, almost stunned. The question had sounded negligent, and it was impossible to read the expression on Vasco's face as he was leaning back in his chair, his face hidden by shadows.

Did he really think, in spite of everything that had happened, that she was still running to Link? Or did he merely want to think so, to salve his own conscience where she was concerned, because if she was going to another man he wouldn't feel so guilty about sending her away?

Anger mingled with the hurt inside her. Well, she was damned if she was going to offer that kind of let-out.

She said quietly, 'I have no firm plans yet.'

'I see.' There was a long silence, then he said, almost grimly, 'It seems you have already guessed what I wanted to say to you.'

Abby looked down at her hands, twisted together in her lap, at the dull golden gleam of her wedding ring.

She said, 'Yes, I've known all along. It's—not the kind of thing you can keep secret, apparently. And if I'd been left in any doubt, Luisa would have settled it for me.'

'Luisa?' He leaned forward, his face set. 'What has she to do with this?'

'More than you think.' She forced herself to smile. 'And you can't imagine I'd want to remain here any longer—in the circumstances.'

'It does not seem to matter what I think,' he said harshly. 'I have been wrong, apparently, from the beginning.' He added almost mockingly, 'I did not realise, *querida* that you had such a practical approach to life.'

His tone did not deceive her. Instinct told her that he was furiously angry. Clearly, his masculine pride had been dinted by her apparent readiness to walk away.

'I also have feelings,' she said evenly. 'Something you seem to have overlooked. I'm not a cipher to be constantly manipulated in any way you think.'

'Is that the impression I have given?' Vasco sounded genuinely horrified. 'Abigail, I promise it is not true...'

'Then you should have let me leave a few weeks ago, when I wanted to,' she said stonily. 'Instead of—riding rough-shod over my wishes as you did.'

There was another silence, then he said. 'But you know why that was. It was a situation—imposed on both of us. I would not have chosen...'

'And nor would I,' Abby interrupted fiercely. 'Well, the situation has now changed drastically in every way, and I want out, Vasco—and the sooner the better!'

He leaned forward, staring at her in the lamp-light as if he had never seen her before. His lips parted, then snapped shut as if he was forcing back whatever he had planned to say. Then, almost wearily, he sent the butt of the cheroot flying over the veranda rail, and stood up.

He said, 'Then it shall be as you wish, Abigail. But may I make one request of you? I have to go to Manaus tomorrow. Would you be good enough to delay your departure until my return?'

She winced. 'Is that necessary?'

His mouth tightened. 'I think so—on practical grounds at least. Presumably you wish to obtain a flight back to Britain. And you will need Pedro Lazaro to fly you out,' he added.

She looked down at the table. 'Very well, then.'

There was another silence, and she thought she heard him sigh faintly, before she heard the sounds of his footsteps walking away from her into the house.

She stayed where she was for long minutes.

So that was it, she thought. It was as simple as that to renounce everything she had ever wanted from life.

That simple—and that heartbreaking.

Three days later, she watched as Pedro Lazaro's aircraft circled above the *fazenda* before disappearing over the trees towards the airstrip.

Since Vasco's departure she had existed in a kind of limbo, but that was over now, and her hours, her very moments at Riocho Negro were numbered.

She hadn't wished to alert the servants by packing in advance, so she supposed that was something she could deal with now. It would give her something to occupy her mind while they were driving over from the airstrip.

She went to the bedroom and removed her suitcase from where it had been stored in the cavernous wardrobe. Then she began to lift her clothes from the rails and drawers, taking immense care to choose only those things she had brought with her.

Suddenly she found herself wondering, as she folded some shirts, whether Della would be accompanying Vasco, or whether he would wait a decent interval—whatever that was—before introducing another woman into the household. She picked up a pair of shoes and rammed them into the case on top of her ill-used garments.

Why was she torturing herself like this? She would know soon enough—and besides, it was hardly any of her business any more. The marriage was over, so why should Vasco bother to dissemble from now on?

She had almost finished her packing when she heard the jeep.

He must have beaten all speed records to get here, she thought bitterly. Was he so keen to get her off the premises? She felt tears pricking at her eyes, and angrily wiped them away with her fists. She was going out of here with her head held high, not snivelling, or worse still, imploring him for the love he could not give her.

She was just fastening her case when he walked into the bedroom. She did not look up as he came to stand beside her, but went on fumbling with the strap on the case which was proving annoyingly recalcitrant.

He said quietly, 'I see you have wasted no time.'

'What did you expect?' Her mouth felt dry. 'Did—did you come back alone?' She despised herself even for asking, but if she had to face Della and her triumph then she needed fair warning.

'Pedro is with me.' Vasco sounded faintly surprised. 'Rosa is giving him some food.'

'I hope he won't be too long.' She got up from her knees and motioned towards the case. 'Could you take that to the veranda for me?'

'Presently,' he said. 'Don't you want to know— haven't you the least curiosity about what took me to Manaus?'

She shook her head. 'I already know.'

'But you don't know the outcome of my visit.' As she tried to move past him, his hands descended on her shoulders, detaining her. He said quietly, 'Abby, I have found a potential buyer for Riocho Negro. I am giving up the struggle here, and going back to Rio to join the family business.' He paused. 'Well, have you nothing to say?'

Abby felt as if she had been turned to stone. She stared up into his face, assimilating the new lines of strain round his mouth and eyes.

She said, half-whispering, 'But you said this was your life—that you'd never leave.'

'And I meant it, then.' Vasco shook his head. 'But since then I have learned that nothing here matters as much as the happiness of the woman I love.'

She tore herself free. She said harshly, 'Then it's a pity you didn't come to this decision a long time ago—and save all this unhappiness and—and bitterness.'

'Is that all you have to say?' There was a note of incredulity in his voice. 'Doesn't it matter to you that I'm prepared to make this sacrifice?'

'What do you expect?' She glared at him. 'A pat on the back, and my heartiest congratulations? Well, forget it. It's no longer my concern what you do, Vasco. I—I hope everything turns out as you want.' She snatched up her case. 'And now I'd like to leave.'

The silence between them was bleak and empty as a desert, then Vasco shrugged and turned away. 'And I was fool enough to think it might make some difference,' he said, half to himself. 'That you would understand why...'

Her voice shook. 'You don't expect much!'

'On the contrary,' he said cynically, 'I expected a great deal. *Adeus, senhora*. I will not keep you any longer.'

Abby hurried through the house, the case banging awkwardly against her legs as she moved. There was no one about, and she was glad of it. She couldn't have borne to face Ana and the others. Vasco could make her excuses when she'd gone, she thought wretchedly, and tell them whatever story he wanted to explain her abrupt departure.

And then, she thought, he would have, somehow, to explain his own.

It crucified her to know that Della had won in the end, although at the same time she knew her cousin would have remained impervious to Riocho Negro's wild, dangerous charm. Vasco was clearly not prepared to risk losing her a second time, and who could blame him?

But he was so committed to the life here, she argued with herself. How could he really be happy in Rio, away from it all, Della's presence at his side notwithstanding?

She had expected Pedro Lazaro to be waiting on the veranda, but there was no sign of him. Abby dumped her case down and stood irresolutely for a moment. It seemed her wait had to continue for a while.

The moments passed with agonising slowness. Don Afonso squawked at her, and she went over and stroked the fierce head with her finger.

'Goodbye, you monster,' she whispered huskily. 'Wish me luck.'

She paused suddenly. I've forgotten the *figa*, she thought. She had always cherished the little wooden token which had welcomed her to Riocho Negro, although it hadn't brought her any real good fortune so far. But maybe its magic wasn't potent enough to prevail against all the adverse influences which had been against her from the first.

But, in spite of that, she didn't want to leave it behind. Apart from anything else, she was aware that it would be the direst ill-luck to abandon it, for any reason.

She went slowly back to the bedroom, hoping and expecting to find it deserted. After all, Vasco had been gone for three days. Even if he was planning to leave, he would have Agnello to see, and paperwork to catch up on.

She pushed open the bedroom door, walked in— then stopped dead.

Because Vasco was there after all. He was sitting on the edge of the bed, holding Abby's discarded nightgown cradled across his body, the expression on his face so agonised that it tore at her soul.

As she watched, transfixed, he lifted the soft, scented folds and buried his face in them with a sound like a sob.

Moving silently, she went to his side and put a hand on his shoulder. 'Vasco?'

He recoiled as if her touch had stung him, flinging the nightgown away and glaring at her in spite of the suspicious moisture in his eyes.

He said tautly, 'What are you doing here? I thought you had gone.'

'I had to come back for something...'

The dark face hardened. He said, with something like contempt, 'Take it, then, and go. Leave me in peace.'

Abby didn't have any idea any more what was going on. She had nothing to follow but instinct. That, and the tormented look she had not been supposed to see.

She said slowly, 'Is that what you want? Is that—really what you want?'

'What do you care? You have told me so often that my dreams, my problems are no longer your concern. In God's name, Abby, have a little mercy, and go quickly,' he added harshly.

She sat down beside him on the bed. Her mouth felt dry. She said, 'What's happened? Has Della—turned you down?'

'Della?' he repeated on a note of incredulity. 'What are you talking about?'

'Please don't pretend, or—lie to me,' she appealed almost feverishly. 'She was in Manaus, and you were with her. Gerulito saw you together, and told everyone.'

Vasco uttered a brief but pungent obscenity. 'That interfering fool!' he said with a snarl. 'What he has cost me!' He flung back his head and looked at her. '*Sim*, she came to Manaus. Her arrival coincided with her letter informing me of her intention, so it was too late to take some kind of avoiding action. But I never intended you should know. Della was only part of the reason for my visit to Manaus, and a very small part.' He paused. 'I saw her once, Abby, in the presence of my lawyer. She was left in no doubt that her journey had been a wasted one, and as far as I am aware, she took the next flight back.'

Abby shook her head. 'That can't be possible,' she protested. 'You wanted me to leave—because of her. You know you did, so don't try and spare my feelings—please.'

'I wanted you to leave?' he repeated slowly. 'What madness is this? What did I ever say—ever do to make you think such a thing? It was always you, *querida*, who wished to go—back to this man who waits for you in England.' His mouth hardened. 'This—Keith.'

'Keith?' she almost shrieked. 'What are you talking about?'

'About the man you love—the man you hoped to marry once, until my—intervention in your life.' Vasco touched her cheek fleetingly. 'Don't look like that, *carinha*. I learned, even before we were married, to live with the fact that your heart did not belong to me.' He shook his head. 'And in Manaus, Della told me that he was still waiting for you, still praying you would return to him. She said the letter he had sent you had begged you to return to England.' His eyes held hers. 'Can you deny that?'

'Yes,' Abby said fiercely, 'I can. I'd never expected to hear from Keith again—and never wanted to either. I'd been seeing him in London, admittedly, but it wasn't serious. I can't imagine why you thought...' She stopped. She said uncertainly, 'Or can I? Did Della—say something?'

'That night when she found us together at your flat,' he said slowly. 'She told me then that you were madly in love with this man Keith, but that he had very little money, so you had gone after me because I could give you more, materially, than he could. She said I would soon find out how mercenary you were.'

'And you believed her?' She gazed at him, stricken.

'What did I really know about you, *carinha*?' His voice gentled. 'Only how sweet you were to love—little more. And I could not escape the idea that you might have given yourself to me out of no more than sexual curiosity.' He cupped her chin in his hand and looked searchingly into her eyes. 'At your uncle's house, long before, you had been—aware of me, hadn't you?'

Flushing, she nodded. 'It was more than that,' she confessed.

'How much more?' The dark gaze held hers gravely.

'Everything in the world,' she said, stumbling a little. 'From the first time I saw you. That's why I left—found a place of my own. But Della knew—Della guessed. She used to—taunt me about it—about the fact that you didn't know I existed. She—threatened to tell you, and I thought she had done—that night. I thought,' she swallowed, 'that was why you'd been so—understanding over the terms of our marriage. That you pitied me...'

'I think you overestimate my capacity for compassion, *querida*.' There was a ghost of laughter in Vasco's voice. 'If I had had the least idea that you were in love with me after all, I would have taken you to bed that night, and every other night that followed. Instead, I told myself to be patient. To wait until we were married, when there would be all the time in the world to woo you, convince you that you were the wife I wanted, and we could be happy together.' He shook his head. 'If I had realised how stubborn you would be about keeping me at arm's length, I would have been in despair, I think.'

Abby said with difficulty, 'But you weren't in love with me. It was Della you wanted . . .'

'My disillusionment with Della had begun long before that night,' Vasco admitted. 'She was beautiful, and she made me want her very badly, without giving anything in return. I told myself that—possessing her would make up for a great deal in other ways, but I was not convinced. It was her own selfish and mercenary attitude that made me wonder whether her accusations about you could be true. I knew what she was capable of, after all, and you were related to her by blood. All the time we were engaged I was waiting, I suppose, for some—taint to show itself. But it never did.'

He was silent for a moment. 'I suppose too that all that time I was falling in love—truly in love, for the first time, although I was too much of a fool to recognise it. I was obsessed with this absurd deadline we had set for ourselves, and how I could get round it. It seemed incredible that I'd gambled my life's happiness on the possibility of some biological fusion having occurred, especially when I did not even believe, myself, that it had happened. When Jorge told me you were pregnant, that day at the settlement, I could have kissed him. In fact, I am not sure I did not.'

'But you were so awful about it,' she protested.

'I was so jealous,' he said softly. 'That first time I saw you with Link, he was touching your hand— something I had hardly permitted myself to do— and I wanted to kill him. I had never felt any such blood-lust towards the man Della left me for. As it was, I stood there, *querida*, watching you with him, and seeing with total clarity at last everything I felt for you. It was—quite a revelation. And afterwards, you never seemed to be out of his company. I wanted to make love to you so badly, to wipe the thought of every other man from your mind. But when I believed I had succeeded, it was only to have you tell me you felt degraded. It seemed then that my love would never be enough for you, and I was too hurt to do anything but hit back.'

'Which you did,' she said, with a little sigh. 'I wanted to die.'

'If it is any consolation, I wanted that too. We had been so close, it was Paradise, then suddenly we were further apart than ever before. The news about the baby gave me fresh hope.' He paused. 'In fact, I had all kinds of hopes. I had been to Manaus that first time principally to try and raise a loan to buy Laracoca, because I knew Gerulito wanted to pull out.' Gently he tucked a strand of hair back behind her ear. 'I thought perhaps you would like to live at Laracoca. The house has all kinds of refinements which this one lacks. I hoped it might reconcile you to staying with me, even if there was no baby.'

Abby's voice shook. 'But when I lost the baby, you said it was "a blessing in disguise".'

His brows drew together. 'But I thought Jorge had spoken to you—told you it was possible there had been something wrong with the baby from the beginning. That sometimes a miscarriage was nature's way of remedying—a mistake.'

'Yes, he did,' she remembered slowly. 'But I didn't understand. I thought you were pleased, because it meant there was nothing to keep us together any more.'

A shudder convulsed his strong body. 'You—thought that?' He shook his head. 'That was the worst day of my life, *querida*—one disaster following upon another. While I was waiting for Jorge to come, all I could think of was Beatriz—and that I might lose you before I had even told you that I loved you.'

'But I told you.' It was as if a veil had been suddenly lifted. 'In the plantation, just before I passed out. It seemed important not to pretend any more, so I said, "I love you".'

'You seemed to be struggling to say something, but you made no sound.' Vasco closed his eyes for a moment. '*Deus*, Abby, it seems we have been fated to misunderstand each other. But at least we can part without recriminations.'

If he'd slapped her, she could not have been more shocked. 'Part?' she echoed stupidly. 'What do you mean?'

'What I say. You are right to go, and I cannot ask you to stay. Because you were quite correct. My life is here, no matter what the hardships. I offered you Rio, as they say a drowning man clutches at a straw, but even as I said it, I knew it would be a disaster for both of us.'

'But I thought you were offering it to Della.' Her words almost fell over themselves. 'I've never wanted Rio—never. I don't care about hardships— I want to stay here with you.' She began to press little kisses to his face. 'You say you love me, and you want to send me away!' she added on a little wail.

His hand tangled in her hair, tipping her face back so he could look at her. He said harshly, 'But leaving was your own idea, Abby, when Luisa told you how much money I had lost through the attack of *largatão*. I cannot blame you, *querida*. I cannot afford now to buy Laracoca, and it will be a struggle to survive.'

'And you think I care about that?' she asked fiercely. 'I'm your wife, Vasco, and I love you. You're not sending me away. I didn't know about the money, I thought you were still in love with Della, and that you wanted to bring her here in my place. I couldn't bear it,' she added, with a little sob. 'Oh, you have to believe me!'

Vasco was silent for a moment, then he said softly, 'So—we fight together to put Riocho Negro back on its feet again. Is that what you truly want?'

'Yes, truly.' Abby was consumed by a happiness, a mounting excitement she had never dreamed could be hers. And a sudden knowledge of her own power too, she realised. She looked at him under her lashes, then lifted her hands to the buttons of his shirt, beginning to slide them from their fastenings. 'Although that isn't all I want,' she murmured huskily.

'Indeed, *senhora*?' His brows lifted, as if he was puzzled. 'I regret I fail to catch your meaning. Perhaps you should be a little more—explicit.'

'It will be my pleasure,' she assured him, her voice smiling. Then she paused abruptly. 'Vasco, what about Pedro Lazaro—he'll still be waiting for me...'

'No, he will have left by now,' Vasco assured her, capturing her hands and returning them to their self-appointed task of ridding him of his clothes. 'I told him that if you had not joined him within twenty minutes, you would be staying.'

'Such arrogance!' she scolded, pausing to run the tip of her tongue along his lower lip. 'You must have been very sure of me.'

Vasco rolled over, pinning her beneath him. 'I was not sure at all,' he said. 'As you know.' He kissed her eyes and the corner of her mouth. 'And I am still waiting, *carinha*, to be convinced.'

Abby said hoarsely, 'Then don't wait any longer—darling, please. Oh God, yes—yes...!'

The urgency which possessed them both was out of control, demanding an instant appeasement. Locked with him, Abby responded out of her own aching need to each forceful thrust of his body, attuned to him, one with him as never before. Their mutual climax was sharp, explosive, almost violent. And afterwards they wept a little, then laughed and kissed the tears away from each other's faces.

'Mine at last!' Vasco exulted, as he cradled her in his arms. 'Mine for ever.'

He fell asleep, and she lay watching him, bewildered by her own joy, revelling in the anticipation of, soon, kissing him awake, enticing him to make love to her again.

She thought about the little *figa* and smiled. It had brought good fortune after all. And in some strange, paradoxical way, even the witch's broom had made its contribution to the harvest of happiness before them.

Life would not be easy, but then it never was, Abby thought drowsily. And at least they would be facing its difficulties together.

Fulfilled and secure, she drifted to sleep in her husband's arms.

Temptation™

TEMPTATION WILL BE
EVEN HARDER TO RESIST...

In September, Temptation is presenting a sophisticated new
face to the world. A fresh look that truly brings Harlequin's
most intimate romances into focus.

What's more, all-time favorite authors Barbara Delinsky, Rita
Clay Estrada, Jayne Ann Krentz and Vicki Lewis Thompson
will join forces to help us celebrate. The result? A very special
quartet of Temptations...

- **Four striking covers**
- **Four stellar authors**
- **Four sensual love stories**
- **Four variations on one spellbinding theme**

All in one great month! Give in to Temptation in September.